Conner put a hand at the small of her back and led her inside the hotel. "I'll stay here tonight. In the lobby. That should give you a peaceful night's sleep."

Adrienne wasn't sure how to respond. She was so grateful for his offer. The thought of having a night of uninterrupted rest made her feel as if a huge weight had been lifted from her shoulders.

But she didn't want him in the lobby. She wanted him in her bed.

Adrienne smiled up at Conner shyly, and reached for his hand. "There's no need for you to stay down here."

He pressed the button for the elevator then stepped close enough to Adrienne that his lips were just inches away from hers.

"I think we both know if I stay up there, a peaceful night's sleep is not what's going to happen."

The elevator door opened but Conner didn't move. Finally Adrienne put a finger on his chest and pushed him back into the elevator and didn't stop until Conner's back was against the elevator's wall.

PRIMAL INSTINCT

—

JANIE CROUCH

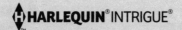
HARLEQUIN® INTRIGUE®

Recycling programs for this product may not exist in your area.

To my mother, the smartest and most well-read person I know. I call you family because I have to, but call you friend because I'm blessed. And to Anu: without your encouragement this book would still be just a file on my computer.

ISBN-13: 978-0-373-69756-4

PRIMAL INSTINCT

Printed in U.S.A.

www.Harlequin.com

ABOUT THE AUTHOR

Janie Crouch loves to read—almost exclusively romance—and has been doing so since middle school. She learned to love Harlequin romance novels when she lived in Wales, U.K., for a few years as a preteen, then moved on to a passion for romantic suspense as an adult.

Janie lives with her husband and four children in southeastern Virginia. Her "day job" is teaching online public speaking and communication courses at a community college. When she's not listening to the voices in her head (and even when she is), Janie enjoys traveling, long-distance running, movie-watching, knitting and adventure/obstacle racing.

Janie tries to live by the anonymous quote "Life is not a journey to the grave with the intention of arriving safely in a pretty and well-preserved body, but rather to skid in broadside, thoroughly used up, totally worn-out and proclaiming, 'Wow, what a ride!'" You can find out more about her at www.janiecrouch.com.

Books by Janie Crouch

HARLEQUIN INTRIGUE
1489—PRIMAL INSTINCT

CAST OF CHARACTERS

Conner Perigo—FBI agent on the trail of a vicious, mocking killer. Willing to do whatever—or use whomever—it takes to stop this murderer from killing again.

Adrienne Jeffries—An ex-profiler for the FBI, with a talent so great she was known as the Bloodhound. She left the bureau years ago with no intention of ever returning. Now she runs a horse ranch in Lodi, California.

"Simon Says"—Serial killer terrorizing the San Francisco area—given this name because of how he signs his notes. Responsible for the death of at least six women so far.

Seth Harrington—Conner's partner and closest friend in the FBI.

Logan Kelly—Chief of the San Francisco FBI field office and a big part of the reason Adrienne left the FBI years ago with no plan to ever return.

Rick Vincent—Manager of Adrienne's horse ranch, with a past and secrets of his own.

Chapter One

FBI agent Conner Perigo knew throwing the file in his hand across the room would be childish and ultimately accomplish nothing except making a mess, but he was still tempted.

Ten months.

Ten months they had been on the trail of this psychopath. Ten months of being two steps behind and watching, helpless, as another woman was murdered. It wasn't in Conner's job description to attend the funerals of women he had never known. That hadn't stopped him from attending one last week. Or three weeks before that. Or a month and a half before that.

Each time he saw one of these women buried, it renewed Conner's determination to catch this bastard.

Five women dead in ten months. Most within a fifty-mile radius of San Francisco, which, of course, had the city in a panic.

"I'm not picking that up, so don't even think about throwing it," Conner's partner and friend, Seth Harrington, said without looking up from his desk.

Conner looked at the file in his hand, then set it down. Maybe flying papers would make him feel better momentarily, but it wasn't worth the aftermath. He sighed. "This case, Seth. I swear I'm about to lose it over this case."

"I hear you, man. It's messed up."

It wasn't just the murders, although those were bad enough. Now the perp was taunting them.

Yesterday the San Francisco FBI field office had received another package. It was the same thing every time. The outside was a box addressed with an innocuous label—like a care package. Of course, innocent-looking or not, each had gone through the extensive FBI bomb scannings and toxic screenings. There was nothing dangerous in any of the packages.

Every delivery was box after box, wrapped in plain brown paper, nested inside each other like one of those Russian dolls. Every time, inside the smallest box, Conner and his team had found a lock of a woman's hair.

And every time, the dead body matching the hair had been found a few days later.

The packages also contained a handwritten note, in third person, with the killer referring to himself as Simon. As if this was all a game of Simon Says.

"Simon says, the FBI is too slow."

"Simon says, you should try harder."

"Simon says, uh-oh, there goes another one."

They had kept all info about the packages from the public, knowing it would cause more of a panic. But around the San Francisco field office, the killer was known as "Simon Says."

There was no doubt about it: this pervert was calling the shots. The game was consistent. The FBI received a package—with zero helpful forensic evidence—then ran around for the next couple of days trying to figure out where the woman was being held with only the city in the return address to go on.

They were always too late. A body would be found somewhere; usually local law enforcement would call it in, and the Bureau would rush to the address. The crime scene, just like the packages, would hold zero helpful forensic evidence.

And then the game would start all over again.

Conner and Seth worked in the FBI's ViCAP division—Violent Criminal Apprehension Program—a subdivision of the Bureau's Behavioral Analysis Unit. Their job was to help law enforcement agencies apprehend violent criminals through investigative analysis. They were the best of the best.

But this killer was always one step ahead of them.

"Perigo, Harrington, my office."

Upon hearing his division chief's words, Conner rubbed his eyes wearily then glanced over to find Harrington looking at him, shaking his head. A trip to Division Chief Logan Kelly's office was never good. The two partners grabbed their notebooks and headed down the hall. The chief took his chair behind his desk and motioned for them to have a seat in the chairs across from him.

"I have spent the entire morning fielding calls. The governor. The deputy director. Even a city councilman. Everybody wants to know the same thing. Where are we on the Simon Says investigation?"

Conner and Seth didn't answer. Chief Kelly knew full well where they were in this investigation: nowhere.

"It's getting a little tiresome explaining over and over that we've got absolutely nothing on this psycho, despite our best efforts."

Conner couldn't agree more, although he didn't say so out loud.

The chief continued, "After talking with the deputy

director this morning, we've decided to pull in some independent contractors to help on the case."

Conner sat up a little straighter in his chair, as did Seth. "Independent contractors, sir? What type?" They had already brought in some outside help on the case—in particular, handwriting experts for the letters. What else could Chief Kelly have in mind?

"Actually we have just one specifically in mind. We want to bring in a…nontraditional profiling expert."

Conner glanced at Seth to find him looking as confused as Conner felt. Why would the department bring in an outsider for profiling? Despite what popular media suggested, there was no actual profiler position at the FBI. All agents were trained in profiling. But just like in all other training—hand-to-hand combat, weapons, languages—an agent could excel at profiling.

Conner and Seth were decent profilers, although both had other specialties. Rarely did the Bureau bring in outsiders unless it was for something very specific. They didn't know enough about Simon Says to bring in someone specific.

And what the hell did Kelly mean by "nontraditional"?

Conner leaned forward. "You and the deputy director have someone specific in mind, sir?"

"Yes, Perigo, we do. Have you ever heard of a profiling expert named Adrienne Jeffries?"

"No." Conner looked over at Seth, who shook his head.

"Perhaps you've heard of the Bloodhound?"

Now Seth spoke up. "Well, yeah, everybody has heard of her. She worked for the Bureau, what? Fifteen, twenty years ago? Had some sort of superpower or something. Could sense and track evil—I don't know. Something like that."

Conner barely refrained from rolling his eyes. Superpowers? Seriously? Didn't they have more important things to do than talk about FBI urban legends from decades ago?

"Adrienne Jeffries last worked for us eight years ago." Chief Kelly pushed a thin file across his desk toward Conner and Seth. "She was hands down the most gifted profiler any of us had ever seen. We want to bring her back in to help with the case."

Conner shrugged, grabbing the file and giving it to his partner without even looking at it. "No offense, Chief, but we have more important things to do than chase down a woman who has been out of the game for a decade."

Seth backed him up. "Yeah, Chief. If she's such a great profiler and can do everything the legend says, why isn't she still on the Bureau's payroll?"

"Ms. Jeffries cut ties with the FBI eight years ago after working with us for two years. During her tenure she was directly accredited with providing critical leads for thirty-seven criminal apprehensions. All over the country. Every team she worked with listed Jeffries as their number one asset and direct link to the arrests."

Seth whistled through his teeth. Conner had to agree. Thirty-seven cases solved in two years was unheard of. It also begged the question: With that success rate, why had she only worked for the FBI for such a short time?

"Why did she quit?" Conner asked.

The older man glanced away for a moment then looked back at Conner. "She decided working with the FBI was not what she wanted to do."

Conner reached over to grab the file Seth was handing to him. He opened it and took a brief glance. There was no picture of Adrienne Jeffries, and half the file was blacked out with thick black lines—making reading the information behind the lines impossible.

Someone very high in the FBI did not want much known about the Bloodhound. Conner couldn't help but be suspicious about so many black marks through a file. Somebody wasn't telling the whole story.

"So for eight years nobody has brought the Bloodhound back in to assist in cases?" Seth asked. "It's been so long, I think everyone just assumed she was dead or too old or not even real to begin with."

"No, she's alive, definitely not too old and very real. We've contacted her a few times over the years, to see if she would resume her contract work, but have been met with a resounding *no* as her answer." Chief Kelly's eyes were cold.

"Why?" Conner looked down at the blacked-out file again. Something was not right in this situation. Not that Conner believed in any of the hocus-pocus junk that surrounded the Bloodhound's reputation. In Conner's opinion cases were solved by hard work and sometimes a little bit of luck, not by superpowers.

"She says she's…not interested in renewing her working agreement with the FBI."

Both Conner and Seth caught the slight hesitation in the chief's statement, but neither said anything.

"Ms. Jeffries has been more interested in maintaining her horse ranch near Lodi."

She was much closer than Conner anticipated. Lodi was only about two hours east of San Francisco. Quite a few vineyards out there and farms, too. And a whole lot of empty space. Definitely a good place for a horse ranch.

"What makes you think she'll be interested in help-

ing us now, if she hasn't been willing to help before?"
Conner asked. Obviously the woman was pretty cold,
if she was as good as they said she was, but refused to
help. Another reason not to waste time on her in Conner's opinion.

"Her circumstances have changed in the past year."

"Does she need money?" Seth asked. Being broke
caused many a change of heart.

"No. She hired a convicted felon as her ranch manager almost a year ago."

Conner leaned back in his chair, confused. "Are they
doing something illegal?"

"No, nothing like that," the chief said. "Her ranch
manager, Rick Vincent, was convicted in the mid-1970s
for breaking and entering. Did three years, was released.
Everything was fine. But he missed his last parole hearing for whatever reason. Warrant's been out for him
since '79."

Conner frowned. "Sorry, Chief, but I don't understand what this has to do with anything. If Vincent
hasn't been arrested since that incident in the '70s,
never had any run-ins with the law at all since then,
it doesn't seem like he would pose much threat to Ms.
Jeffries now."

The chief tilted his head. "No, we're not worried
about him being a threat to her. Reports indicate they
are actually pretty friendly with each other."

Conner frowned over at Seth. *Reports indicate?*
What was going on here?

Seth shrugged, obviously as confused as Conner.

"Reports, sir?" Conner asked. "Has she been under
surveillance?"

"Not surveillance, exactly. Just attempts on our part,
from time to time, to get her to return and provide pro-

filing assistance." The chief looked down at his desk and began reorganizing papers, obviously not wanting to provide too much information about the reports or meetings with Ms. Jeffries.

It was damn strange, if anyone asked Conner. He waited for the chief to get to the point he was so long in coming to.

Chief Kelly finally looked up from his desk. "I want you to go out to Adrienne Jeffries's horse ranch and ask for her help with the case. And if she says no, then I want you to use the arrest of Rick Vincent as a threat to get her cooperation."

It was all Conner could do to keep from jumping out of his chair. He heard Seth make some sort of incredulous sound next to him. *"What?* Chief, that's pretty much blackmail."

The chief's eyes narrowed. "No, Perigo. It's doing your job. She has a criminal on her property, and you need to bring him in."

"A nonviolent criminal with a B&E rap from more than thirty years ago. No law enforcement agency would waste the gas out to Lodi to pick up Vincent!" Seth exclaimed. He didn't like this any more than Conner.

"Rick Vincent is not the primary objective here, obviously. Adrienne Jeffries's cooperation is."

"Chief…" Conner's cajoling tone was cut off before he could get a second word out.

"Perigo, I get it. You don't like the tactics. Fine, they're not my favorite, either. But how many more women are you willing to let die, when we have a known tool at our disposal? A tool proven to get results?"

Conner sat in silence. He didn't agree with Chief Kelly's orders. Hell, he didn't even believe Adrienne

Jeffries could possibly be as useful as everyone said. But regardless, if it meant catching Simon Says and saving even one woman's life, he was willing to try.

"All right, Chief. We'll go see her tomorrow morning."

A FEW HOURS later, long after the office began emptying and most of the other agents were gone, Conner and Seth sat at their desks. Conner reached into his bottom drawer and pulled out a toy baseball made of a foamy material. He leaned back in his chair and put his feet on the desk, tossing the ball up in the air and catching it on its way back down. Seth saw him and leaned back in his own chair.

They had spent every moment since leaving Chief Kelly's office going back over the details of the Simon Says case. They had read through the testimony of local law enforcement again, pored over the lives of the victims to see if they could find any commonalities once more, reviewed crime scene video footage and photos additionally, as well.

It had led to nothing.

Conner had hoped to find something—anything—that would keep them from having to bring in Adrienne Jeffries tomorrow. He wasn't interested in her help, and he wasn't comfortable with the means they were using to get it.

Conner tossed the ball over to Seth. "This whole Adrienne Jeffries thing just doesn't feel right, if you ask me."

Seth caught the ball easily. "Chief Kelly seems legitimately convinced that she can help us."

"Yeah."

"But you don't think so."

"I think this is a waste of time. I think this lady was probably hot back in the day, and maybe she and Kelly had a relationship or something."

"You think she snowed him." Seth tossed the ball back.

"Look, I'm really not trying to talk bad about anybody, but I don't believe in mind reading or telepathy or superheroes to solve cases."

And dragging some middle-aged woman from her *horse farm* in the middle of Nowhere, California, into a case of this magnitude was not Conner's idea of good situational management. Conner threw the ball to Seth.

"You know, there have been documented cases of nontraditional methods actually working."

Conner dragged a hand through his black hair making it even more scruffy-looking than usual. "I don't even want to hear it, Harrington. I'm pissed. I'm pissed that we're wasting time going all the way out there."

"As opposed to doing what?" Seth interjected. "Sitting around the office waiting for the perp to drop off another package?"

Conner leaned his head back and closed his eyes, sighing. Seth had a point. If this lady could help them break open the case in some way, Conner would take it. But he planned to be very careful about what info she was given. He wasn't sure if she had tricked Chief Kelly and the other agents in some way before, but she damn well wouldn't fool Conner.

"Fine," Conner said. "But I would just like it stated, for the record, that I am going there under direct orders. I do not believe this to be the most effective use of our time."

Seth nodded. "Duly noted, counselor." He tossed the ball back to Conner.

Conner laid the ball on his desk and picked up Adrienne Jeffries's ridiculously short and useless file. When he had tried to run her info in the Bureau's computer system, the same thing happened. Somebody pretty high up in the FBI—maybe even higher than Chief Kelly—was protecting her or hiding something. There was no picture, no physical description of the woman, no mention of her ability and definitely no use of the word *bloodhound*.

By looking at her file, she could've been one of thousands of contractors who had worked as support staff for the FBI. Everything from janitorial to catering, clerking to photographing, were hired out each year. Every single one of those people had a file at the Bureau.

The fact that so much was blacked out in Adrienne Jeffries's file was an immediate giveaway that she was no clerk or anything so benign. Basically her name and the years she'd worked for the Bureau were the only info the file provided.

It was what wasn't provided that concerned Conner. If she was such a gifted profiler, why wasn't Jeffries helping the FBI anymore? What type of person would turn their back on an ability like that, if it would save lives? A cold and uncaring one, to be sure.

And why the heck had she been under "not surveillance, exactly"? Contract workers quit the FBI all the time. Most were not being watched by the Bureau, as far as Conner knew. But this woman was, at least partially.

There was something not right about this situation and this woman. The one thing of which Conner was confident was that he did not have all the data. He loosened the top button of his shirt under his tie and grabbed the ball again, tossing it to Seth.

Conner did not like going into any situation blind.
But it seemed like he didn't have much choice in this
case. They would bring the woman in, as he had been
ordered, glean any useful info, if any, and then would
get back to real work.

This was a waste of his time.

Chapter Two

The next morning, as they arrived at Adrienne Jeffries's ranch, Conner was even more certain this trip was a waste of time. He could admit to himself that the ranch was picturesque among the rolling hills in Lodi but still resented having to come here. A modest-sized house sat in the middle of multiple corralled areas. A barn—at least the same size as the house, maybe even a bit bigger—sat a few hundred yards back from the house.

"Let's get this over with," Conner muttered.

They parked and walked up the three worn steps to the wraparound porch. Although the porch and its furniture was well kept, everything was obviously old and secondhand. Conner knocked on a door that could use another coat of paint. No one answered.

"Let's try the barn," Seth suggested, heading back down the steps.

That the barn was in a much better state than the house seemed to be immediately evident. Well maintained, organized, all repairs up-to-date. Evidently any money the horse ranch made went back into the barn first.

Conner could hear a man talking inside the barn, although couldn't make sense of what he was saying. Both Conner and Seth were immediately on alert.

"Hello in the barn! This is FBI Special Agents Conner Perigo and Seth Harrington," Conner called.

The talking immediately stopped, but there was no response.

"Sir? We're looking for a Ms. Adrienne Jeffries. We would like to come in the barn."

A muttered curse, then what sounded like chewing tobacco being spit. "Fine. Come on in," the man in the barn finally replied.

"Sir, is it just you in the barn?" Seth asked as he and Conner entered slowly.

"Yes."

"Are you sure? We heard you talking to someone."

"Yeah, I was talking to Willie Nelson, but I'm pretty sure he's not going to be talking back anytime soon."

Willie Nelson? Conner and Seth glanced at each other again as they walked farther in, both with hands near their weapons. As their eyes adjusted to the dimness of the barn, Conner saw the man was referring to a horse he was brushing inside a stall.

The man was in his mid-sixties, short and wiry. As he walked around the horse, Conner noticed he moved with a limp in his left leg. This had to be Rick Vincent.

"I'm Agent Perigo. This is Agent Harrington. We're from the FBI."

"Yeah, I heard you the first time." The older man was obviously not a big fan of law enforcement. "I'm busy."

"We're looking for Ms. Jeffries, sir. She owns this ranch, correct?" Seth asked, moving a couple steps to the left, subtly blocking the exit, should the older man try to run.

"Yeah, she owns it. She's not here right now."

"Not here on the ranch or not here in the barn?" Conner asked when the man didn't offer any more info.

"She's off riding one of the horses."

"And may we ask your name, sir?" Although they already knew.

"Vincent. Rick Vincent," the man offered after a hesitation. Conner could see he was trying to judge how much they knew about him.

"You work here, Mr. Vincent?" Conner asked.

"Just Vincent. Yeah, I work here. I'm the ranch manager."

"How long have you worked here?" Seth asked.

"Just about a year now."

"Ms. Jeffries owned the place the entire time?"

Conner let Seth ask the questions while Conner observed the man and the barn. They already knew the answers, but they could learn a lot by what someone was willing to lie about.

"Yeah."

"Just you and her working here?"

"Yeah. Although we get some kids from the 4-H Club who come in on weekends and stuff like that. And some horticultural students from the local community college every once in a while."

"May I get your address, Vincent? Just in case we need to talk to you again after we speak to Ms. Jeffries."

Vincent paused so long Conner thought he might not answer at all. "I live in the house here."

Conner glanced at Seth with an eyebrow raised. "So you live with Ms. Jeffries in the house?" *Interesting.*

"Yes."

"And it's just the two of you?"

"It's not like what you boys are thinking. We both

live in the house, but it's not like that." Vincent glared at them both, then spat to the side again.

Okay, maybe not romantic, but protective. Still interesting.

Seth seemed about to ask another question when a female voice from outside the barn interrupted him.

"Vince! I officially love Ruby Tuesday! I so hope the owners end up boarding her here. Maybe I should offer a discount just so I can see this pretty girl all the time." A burst of joyful laughter drew Conner's focus.

The woman's voice faded as she started talking to the horse, obviously common practice around here.

A moment later a woman in her mid-twenties— probably one of the college students Vincent had mentioned—led Ruby Tuesday into the barn. She stopped, noticeably shocked when she saw Conner and Seth. She looked at Vincent with concern then rubbed her head and took a few steps back.

"You okay, kiddo?" Vincent asked.

The young woman looked almost panicked. Conner stepped toward her with his arms held out in a soothing manner. "We didn't mean to startle you, miss. My name is Agent Perigo. This is Agent Harrington."

"You're FBI," she stammered out, still panicky. Did everyone here have an aversion to the FBI?

Conner smiled and tried to reassure the young woman. "Yes. We're actually looking for Adrienne Jeffries. Mr. Vincent said she was riding. Did you happen to see her while you were out?"

The woman took a deep breath and rubbed her head again. She looked at Vincent, then back at Conner. But she didn't respond.

Seth decided to take a shot. "We can assure you Ms.

Jeffries isn't in any trouble. We were just hoping to talk to her for a bit."

The young woman took a couple of breaths and seemed to compose herself. "Okay."

Seth looked at Conner, who shrugged, then asked, "Okay, what?"

"Okay, I'm here. You can talk to me."

Conner could feel the shock rolling over him. This *could not* be the Adrienne Jeffries they were supposed to contact. She was too young, with her pixie-short hair and big brown eyes.

She was too damn beautiful.

"No." Conner denied it before he could help himself. "Your mom, maybe? Is there another Adrienne Jeffries at this address?"

The young woman sighed and shook her head. "Nope, just me." She led the horse over to Vincent and gave him the reins. "Let's go inside the house to talk. I think we'll be more comfortable."

"I'll come, too," Vincent was quick to interject.

Conner watched as Adrienne laid a gentle hand on the older man's arm. Obviously the protectiveness went both ways. He felt a little guilty that they were about to use that protectiveness against her.

"I'm fine, Vince, I promise." Adrienne smiled at Vincent then turned to look directly at Conner. "If they're FBI, I know why they're here."

There was definitely no smile when she said that. Vincent was obviously reluctant but agreed.

Adrienne Jeffries silently walked out of the barn, leaving Conner and Seth to follow, or just as obviously not to follow. They made their way behind her wordlessly. Conner couldn't help admiring how well she filled out her worn jeans as she walked ahead of them.

They obviously weren't designer jeans, but who the hell cared if she looked like that in them?

Seth reached over and nudged him with his elbow.

"What?" Conner whispered, reluctantly drawing his eyes away from Adrienne's jeans.

"I don't have a *hankie* so I'm offering you my sleeve."

"What the hell are you talking about?"

"To wipe the drool from your mouth, man. You missed some."

Conner thought just a moment about gut-punching his partner before reaching the house but decided it wasn't worth it. He wasn't *drooling,* for God's sake.

But his eyes were drawn back to her jeans one more time.

Adrienne Jeffries was definitely not some middle-aged woman who had worked for the Bureau a decade ago. Something was not adding up between what Chief Logan Kelly had told them and what Conner was seeing with his own eyes.

If she had been the Bloodhound for the FBI, then she would have been a teenager when it had happened. He knew that couldn't be right. Something did not fit in this situation.

Adrienne made her way through the back door, not gesturing for the men to follow, but at least not slamming the door behind her. Conner and Seth followed her and found themselves in the kitchen. The room, like everything else they'd seen on the ranch—the front porch, the steps, the barn, *her jeans*—Conner quickly pushed that thought away—was clean but worn.

Adrienne crossed over to the sink, filled a glass with water and drank it down without stopping. Only afterward did she place the glass on the counter and turn to face them.

"Have a seat." She gestured to the four chairs at the kitchen table. Conner took one and Seth took the one across from him.

Adrienne stayed where she was with her back against the sink counter. She didn't offer them a drink or any food. Nor did she offer them any information. She didn't exactly glare, but her gaze definitely wasn't inviting. Conner reclined in his chair and returned the almost hostile look.

If this was the way she wanted to play it, that's how he would play it.

Seth noticed Conner's angry expression and sighed. They had played Good Cop–Bad Cop many times over the years, but it was usually Conner who was the good cop. He had a way of putting people at ease when he wanted to. But looking at the woman staring at him so haughtily, Conner had no desire to play good cop today.

"Ms. Jeffries," Seth took over, "we'd like to ask you a few questions about your…contract work for the FBI."

"What about it?" Adrienne spoke to Seth but continued to glare at Conner. Conner glared back.

Seth sighed again. "Can you tell us the nature of the work you did for the Bureau?"

Adrienne finally looked over at Seth, her stance softening a bit. "Why don't you tell me what you know, and I'll fill in some gaps."

Conner cut in. "How old are you?"

The glare was back at him now. "Didn't your mother ever teach you that is a rude question? Besides, I'm sure you have a fancy FBI file on me with that sort of information."

Seth smiled engagingly. "You'd be surprised at how sparse your file is."

Some of the heat left Adrienne's eyes. "I'm twenty-eight."

Conner shook his head. That could not be right. "Are you sure?" he demanded more gruffly than he intended. He heard Seth sigh again.

"Am I sure?" All the hostility was back. "Am I sure how old I am? Wait, let me get out all my fingers and toes so I'm sure I haven't miscounted."

"I didn't mean that. I just mean, now is not the time to lie about your age for vanity's sake or some such nonsense."

"I am quite sure of how old I am and have no need to lie about it. Twenty-eight."

Seth jumped in, obviously trying to instill some reason into the situation. "I think what my partner means, Ms. Jeffries, is that, if you are twenty-eight years old and worked for the FBI ten years ago, that would've made you pretty young."

Adrienne looked away but not before Conner saw shadows looming in her eyes. "Let's just say the FBI made a special exception in my case." She walked over and got her wallet from a purse hanging on a wall hook. She took out her driver's license and threw it down on top of the table.

"Twenty-eight." Seth glanced at it then slid the license over to Conner.

She wasn't lying. He supposed the ID could be forged, but it didn't seem like there was much purpose to it.

That meant she had been *eighteen years old* when she'd been the Bloodhound for the FBI. No wonder all the information was blacked out in that damn file.

"Still rude to ask," Adrienne muttered under her breath from back at her perch at the sink.

Conner knew he should apologize but couldn't bring himself to do it. Twenty-eight or not, this woman was getting under his skin.

Seth attempted to start again. "Obviously there's a lot we don't know, Ms. Jeffries. If you would be willing to help us fill in the holes, this would probably be a lot easier on all of us."

"Please, call me Adrienne, Agent Harrington." The invitation was very obviously not extended to Conner.

"Thanks, Adrienne. And you're welcome to call me Seth." She smiled sweetly at Seth, and Conner thought he might have to jump out of his chair and stand between the two of them. Neither of them seemed to notice his strange behavior, thank God. He needed to calm the hell down.

"Could you tell us what you did for the FBI?" Seth asked her with a smile that had Conner ready to jump up again.

Calm. Down. What in the world was the matter with him?

"I'm sure you've heard rumors. I have a special talent. I can profile evil very well."

Seth nodded. "Exactly how did you use your talent to help the Bureau?"

"The closer I am to a person with malicious intent, the more clearly I can sense what the person is thinking. And I don't have to be near the actual person. I can be around something he or she has touched or been near and be able to 'read' the evil."

"Bloodhound," Conner muttered under his breath, shaking his head. He still didn't believe any of it.

"Yes, it's an accurate description, I suppose." Adrienne's smile was rueful. "Although I was glad nobody ever called me that to my face. Teenage girls don't respond well to being told they're like a dog."

Conner still did not like this teenager talk. He planned to have a discussion about Adrienne with Chief Kelly as soon as possible.

"So you're a psychic? Or an empath or something like that?" Harrington asked gently, although his doubts crept into his tone.

"No, not really. I don't have superpowers. I can't read people's minds or anything. I don't feel what other people are feeling. Like, if you were sad right now, I wouldn't feel your sadness. Really it's just evil I feel, malicious intent. It's kind of like they draw me into their thoughts."

"Why? How?" Conner didn't attempt to hide his incredulity at all.

"I don't know. Some people are terribly sensitive to heat or light. My brain is just sensitive to negative energy."

"Do you feel it about everybody?"

"No. Most people aren't menacing. They can be catty and rude, but usually it's due to their own insecurity rather than actual malevolence."

"So how do you 'sense' it? Do you see images? Have visions?" Seth asked.

"Hear little voices in your head?" Conner tagged on.

Adrienne ignored Conner. "The closer I am to the person—in terms of physical proximity—the clearer I can sense everything. From far away it's like seeing and hearing through multiple panes of glass—difficult to make out the details. If I am close, it's like being inside someone's head. I can see and hear everything."

Conner didn't believe any of this. "So what if I want you to demonstrate your 'powers'? Can you do that?"

Adrienne's irritated gaze swung around to Conner again. "Not really."

"Well, that's pretty convenient, isn't it?" Conner snapped.

More glaring was shared between Adrienne and Conner. "It's not a dog and pony show, Special Agent Jackass."

That got a snicker from Seth.

"And no offense, but I don't owe you anything."

Conner stood up before he was even aware of what he was doing and took a step toward Adrienne. What was it about this one tiny woman that made him feel like he was about to jump out of his own skin?

Fortunately Seth waylaid him before he had a chance to… Conner had no idea what he would've done when he reached Adrienne.

"Adrienne, can you excuse us for a moment? I need to discuss a text I just received with Agent Perigo out on the porch."

Seth grabbed Conner's arm—hard—and began pushing him through the small living room and out the front door.

"What?" Conner barked at him the moment the door was closed.

"You're asking *me* what?" There was obviously no text Seth wanted to show him. "I was just wondering if you wanted to arrest her. Maybe you've got her fingered as our killer."

"What?" Conner felt like a parrot.

"Well, the way you've been treating her, Agent *Jackass,* is like she's a perp, or at the very least some sort of hostile witness."

Conner rubbed his hand over his face wearily. Everything Harrington was saying was true.

"I don't know what the hell's the matter with me, Seth."

"I don't know either, but you've got to get yourself under control. She's not the bad guy here."

"I know."

"You think this is a waste of time, Con, I get that. And to be honest, I don't know what to believe, either. But if what she's saying—what Chief Kelly said—is true…"

"Then it could really be the break in the case we've been hoping for," Conner finished for him.

"You don't like her, for whatever reason. Fine. But let's see what she can do."

Conner almost corrected Seth but stopped. It wasn't that he didn't like Adrienne Jeffries—he hadn't made up his mind whether he liked the little spitfire or not. But liking or disliking didn't really seem to matter. He was *affected* by her. And it made him damn uncomfortable.

"All right, I'll behave."

Seth looked relieved. "Good."

They walked back through the door and into the kitchen.

"Saving the world one text at a time?" Adrienne asked with one brow cocked. She had taken a seat at the table in the chair farthest away from where Conner had been sitting.

"Something like that." Seth smiled.

Conner didn't say anything. He figured opening his mouth would just get him in trouble.

"You two must be on some pretty big case for the FBI to put you at my doorstep after all these years."

"We are. It's gruesome," Seth informed her.

"And you were told I could help."

Both men nodded.

Adrienne continued. "And when they sent you out here to bring me back, did they warn you I would tell you to go screw yourselves?"

Chapter Three

Adrienne could not believe it was all happening again.

She would not let the FBI just walk in and take over her life. She was older now, wiser. And she knew the toll using her gift to help the FBI would take. She had lived through it before.

Barely.

She knew Special Agent Friendly and his sidekick Special Agent Hot-But-Annoying sitting at her kitchen table really had no idea what her gifts were or what her life had been like ten years ago when she had worked for the Bureau.

Worked. Adrienne barely restrained a bark of laughter. More like *duped and manipulated.*

She knew Agent Hot, *excuse me,* Agent *Perigo* was particularly skeptical. Adrienne wasn't offended by that. But there was something about him that made her slightly crazy. She had spent the past twenty minutes itching to slap the alternating smug and hostile looks off his face. Either that or jump his bones.

Adrienne had been downright shocked when she had returned Ruby Tuesday to the barn and found the two men standing there with Vincent. Whenever someone unfamiliar was around, Adrienne could always sense it.

Unless they had some sort of malevolent side, she couldn't see their thoughts, but everyone—good or bad—gave off some sort of buzz that she picked up on in her brain. With familiar people she had learned to ignore it, the way someone ignores the slight sound a computer or TV makes when it's on but has no volume. Just the slightest buzz. The more people that were around, the louder the buzz.

But Adrienne had heard nothing when she had walked into the barn. That's why she had been so shocked to see the agents—she hadn't heard their buzz.

Nothing. As a matter of fact, she still couldn't hear it.

But they were here, and they wanted her help. She couldn't afford to help them. The best thing she could do, she knew, was be cold and turn them away. But looking at Agent Perigo, she knew turning them away would not be easy.

"Guys, I appreciate that you've come all the way out here. But Chief Kelly shouldn't have sent you. Whatever your case is, I can't help you."

"Adrienne…" Agent Harrington began in a cajoling tone.

"Can't or won't?" Perigo interrupted Harrington and got right to the point.

The urge to slap Perigo was itching its way through Adrienne's palm again. "I have responsibilities here."

"The FBI would more than compensate you for your time. Plus, don't you have Vincent to run things for you if you're gone?" Perigo continued.

"It's not just that," Adrienne backpedaled.

"Then what is it, Adrienne?" Seth asked in a concerned voice. He sounded completely sincere. Adrienne wondered for a moment if he practiced that voice.

"There's a discomfort that comes with using my

gift." That was putting it ridiculously mildly. "Plus, like I said, I can't—or am not willing to—uproot my life. I'm needed here."

Adrienne watched as the two men looked at each other across the table, communicating without speaking. Obviously there was a plan B, although it looked as though both of them found the thought of it distasteful.

"Adrienne, we were sent here by our superiors with a directive to obtain your cooperation in our case." Agent Harrington paused, but she knew his statement wasn't finished. She didn't have long to wait. "By any means available to us."

Adrienne looked at Harrington, then Agent Perigo, confused. "'Any means available?' Are you planning on making me leave the ranch at gunpoint?"

"No. Nothing so drastic, I assure you," Harrington responded with a smile. "But our instructions are to either bring you back with us or bring in your ranch manager, Mr. Vincent."

"Why Vince? What does he have to do with this?"

Agent Perigo interjected, "Do you make a practice of hiring and cohabiting with convicted felons or fugitives on your ranch?"

"What?" Adrienne expressed her shock before she could help herself. Not a good logistical move.

"So you're unaware of Mr. Vincent's past history and that he is currently wanted in the state of Nevada for parole violation?"

Adrienne shook her head. "I knew he had some trouble with the law a while ago. But he never offered much information about it, and I never asked."

Harrington leaned toward her. "Isn't it dangerous to work and live with a man you know so little about?"

Adrienne smiled grimly. She had never been concerned about her safety with Vince—she had known from the beginning he meant her no harm. That was one of the few good things about her gift. "Let's just say that my talent makes me an excellent judge of character. Vince would never harm me."

Agent Perigo sighed. "Regardless. Our instructions are clear. We're either to bring you in or bring Rick Vincent in. You choose."

Adrienne could feel temper rising up through her body. Obviously nobody in the FBI had changed in the past decade. They still didn't care who they used—or used up—to get what they wanted.

"Common blackmail? Is that what the FBI has resorted to?" It was all she could do to keep her fist from banging down on the table.

Harrington reached a hand out toward her, but she jerked back in her seat. "Ms. Jeffries."

At least he had the sense to revert to last names if they were going to use blackmail.

"We have to uphold the law. There is a warrant out for Mr. Vincent's arrest."

"That you will conveniently overlook if I agree to help the FBI on the case."

Agent Harrington cleared his throat. "Let's just say, if we had your help on the case, we would probably be so busy, we may totally forget we even saw Rick Vincent here."

Adrienne was too angry to say anything. She did not want to be forced back into helping the FBI but couldn't stand the thought of Vincent going to prison. The older man had no evil in him whatsoever. Whatever crime he had committed, it was in a past far behind him. Now he was kind and helpful and wonderful with the horses, if a little gruff with people.

They sat in silence for long moments. Adrienne had no idea what the FBI agents were thinking, but they wisely did not give voice to their thoughts. She glanced at Harrington first but found him looking down at his hands. She then glanced over at Agent Perigo with hesitation, unsure of what she would find.

He met her eyes directly. Instead of the hostility she had expected to see, she found sincerity and the slightest hint of compassion. No matter what he thought of her abilities, or her personally, he obviously found this stalemate distasteful.

And he had the most gorgeous green eyes she had ever seen. Just the slightest hint of gold in them. For the first time Adrienne wished she had met Agent Perigo under different circumstances. Wished he didn't work for an organization that was sure to leave her broken by the time this was all over.

Adrienne looked away from Agent Perigo's piercing eyes and down at her kitchen table. She couldn't see any way out of this. She wasn't going to let anything happen to Vincent, as long as there were any other options. Plus she was older now, wiser, more able to protect herself from the FBI. Because she had no doubt that what had happened before, ten years ago, would happen again if she wasn't careful. The solution was making sure it didn't repeat itself.

Of course she had no idea how to do that.

She looked up from the scarred kitchen table, hoping she didn't resemble it by the time this was all over.

"Okay, fine. I'll help you."

An hour later, just before lunch, Adrienne watched Agents Perigo and Harrington drive away. She had been given instructions about where and when to report tomorrow, and had assured them she would be there.

Then, just before leaving, Agent Perigo made a special trip out to the barn to say goodbye to Vincent. All for Adrienne's benefit.

Jackass. Obviously, she had been mistaken about any compassion she had seen in him.

Vince immediately knew something was up.

"That FBI agent came out to the barn to say goodbye to me," the older man stated as he washed his hands for lunch. "Seemed a mite odd."

Adrienne rolled her eyes. "Yeah, I know. If it helps, I think it was a gesture meant for me, not you."

"We never really talked much about you working for the FBI."

Adrienne began making each of them a sandwich. "I worked for them briefly years ago. It wasn't a pleasant experience. Not something I discuss much."

"I've found, in my general experience, that anything having to do with law enforcement is not a pleasant experience."

Adrienne smiled at that. Although her and Vince's experiences with law enforcement were different, the resulting feelings were the same.

"And now they want you to come back and work for them again?" the older man asked.

Adrienne slapped mustard onto the sandwich and rubbed it around with more force than necessary. "That pretty much sums it up."

"But you don't want to go back to work for them."

"My life is here. My responsibilities are here." More mustard was slapped on the other piece of bread.

"Well now, you know I can handle everything around here if you needed to go off somewhere. This place isn't so big that one person can't hold down the fort for a while. You did it for long enough before I came along."

"I know you can handle it, Vince. I'm not sure what I would've done without you for the past year." She smiled gently at him.

The older man blushed and looked away. Nothing thrilled Vince less than talking about feelings, Adrienne knew.

"Vince, I know you had trouble with the law in your past, but I've known from the beginning that you were someone I could trust. Whatever happened in the past isn't important to me. You've been a godsend." She handed him a sandwich.

"Well, you know that goes both ways." Vince took a big bite of his sandwich and chewed thoughtfully. "Why do I get the feeling all of this conversation has to do with those FBI agents?"

Adrienne sighed. "It looks like I'm going to need you to keep things afloat for me here for a little bit."

"While you go help the FBI."

"Yeah."

"What exactly do you, or did you do, for them?"

Adrienne pushed her sandwich around on her plate. How was she supposed to explain this? "I guess I was kind of a profiler for them."

Vince grunted in agreement the way he often did. He didn't look at all surprised. "I figured it was something like that, given your…" He waved his hand in circles above his head.

Adrienne was shocked. She had no idea Vince was aware of her gift. They had never talked about it. "You knew?"

"Not at first. As a matter of fact, when you initially hired me, I thought you were a little reckless. What woman hires someone completely unknown, then invites him a few weeks later to move into the house with her?"

"Vince, you were sleeping out in the barn!"

"I know, I know. Don't get me wrong. I am grateful for your invite. But I could've been dangerous." Vince shook his head.

"I knew you weren't."

Vince grunted in agreement again. "Then I saw over the next few months how patient you were with almost everybody. Even some of the brattiest or angriest kids who came out here to work. You were always kind and gentle, when I wanted to throw some of them out on their ears."

Vince put down his sandwich and looked Adrienne right in the eye. "Then that blond guy showed up last July. He seemed polite and charming. All the college girls were sighing over him and his good looks. You came out of the house, glanced at him for five seconds, and asked him to leave and never come back."

Adrienne remembered very clearly the appearance of the young man, probably twenty or twenty-one years old. Like Vince said, he had blond hair, blue eyes—all-American good looks. Seemed amiable and charismatic, at least on the outside.

But the thoughts in his mind were utterly sinister. A malevolence that only Adrienne could pick up on had permeated the air around the young man. The things he thought of doing to the female students who had worked at Adrienne's ranch—to Adrienne herself, once he had seen her—made Adrienne's stomach churn. She had immediately made him leave, much to the girls' dismay, telling him there were no more internships available.

Then had promptly gone back inside and vomited the entire contents of her stomach.

The next day Adrienne had gone into town to check with the sheriff's office to see if there were any warrants out for the man or any reported attacks on women in the area. There were none. Adrienne decided to leave it alone—after all, she had no idea if he would ever act on any of those evil instincts floating around in his brain. Perhaps not. But either way she did not want him around her ranch or the young people she had working there. Thankfully they never saw him again.

Adrienne looked at Vince. "Yeah. I remember him."

"I don't know why you sent him away. I don't know why you made him—a good, clean-cut-looking kid— leave when you had hired some of the roughest-looking tattooed hoodlums multiple times. Hell, I'd seen you *make* jobs for people when we didn't need another soul."

"He just wasn't a good fit for our ranch."

"It's your ranch, and you can certainly hire or not hire anyone you see fit. But you not even giving that kid a chance—that kind of caught my attention."

Vince stood and walked his plate over to the sink, then continued. "I watched you after that when you were around people—especially new folk. It took a while, but I realized you have a sort of insight into people that most don't have."

Adrienne sat in silence as Vince rinsed his plate off, then turned to look at her. "It's probably more than just an insight if the FBI wants your help."

"A little. Especially when it comes to anyone who has some sort of sinister intent. I can kind of hear their thoughts." Adrienne was worried that she may be freaking Vince out, but he seemed to take it all in stride.

"Hmm. And you helped the FBI before?"

"Yes."

"You must have been pretty young."

"Barely eighteen."

Vince's eyes narrowed at that. "Hmm. And working with them wasn't a pleasant experience?"

"That's putting it mildly."

Vince nodded. "But you're going back to work for them?"

Adrienne looked away; she didn't want Vince to know he was the reason she was returning to work for the FBI. "Yeah."

"Even though you don't want to." It wasn't a question.

"Pretty much."

"And you told them you're not interested in helping?"

"I tried."

"But they didn't listen?"

"Evidently they need my help in a pretty big way. 'No' wasn't a possibility for an answer."

"Seems to me, living in this free country of ours, no is always a possibility in a situation like this."

Adrienne finished her sandwich and brought her plate to the sink so she wouldn't have to look at Vince. "Well, let's just say they made me an offer I couldn't refuse."

There was silence for long moments, and Adrienne made the mistake of looking over at the older man.

"If I told you," Vince began with a grimace, "I had missed my last few meetings with my parole officer after I left prison, and that there's a warrant out for my arrest, would this be new information to you?"

Adrienne looked back down at the plate she was washing. "I already told you, Vince. I don't care what happened in the past. I just know I can trust you now," she sidestepped.

Vince nodded. "But that's not what I asked you."

Adrienne sighed. "No, that info isn't new to me."

"Did you know this before today?"

Adrienne turned and looked the older man in the eye. "No. Agents Perigo and Harrington told me."

"And that's how they're getting you to come back, right? By using me?"

"Vince..." Adrienne reached toward him but he leaned back in his chair away from her.

"I won't let you do it, you understand? I'm not going to let you be forced into something because of me!"

"Vince, it's all right. I'm going to do this one thing for them, and that will be the end of it. And before I do, I'll get their assurance that the warrant for you will be canceled or whatever. I promise. It's not a big deal."

"I still don't like this," Vince muttered.

"Don't worry. I'm going to be fine. Maybe I'll find that the FBI has become a little better at playing with others in the past ten years."

Vince took a sip of his drink and sat back in the chair. "I wouldn't hold your breath."

Chapter Four

Hours later Conner lay sprawled in his bed looking up at the ceiling. After leaving Adrienne Jeffries's house, he had been pretty much useless for the rest of the day. They had gone back to the office for a couple of hours, briefly reporting to Chief Kelly about their success with getting Adrienne's agreement to help. Seth, well aware of Conner's black mood, had talked Conner out of questioning the chief about Adrienne's history with the FBI.

There were so many things about Adrienne Jeffries's history that didn't add up that Conner didn't know where to even begin his questioning. Definitely better to leave his questions until he was in a better—or at least more respectful—frame of mind. Maybe he would just talk to her and leave the chief out of it altogether. Less chance of Conner getting fired that way.

Adrienne definitely had not been what he was expecting. For one, her age. Certainly not the middle-aged woman he had been anticipating. But that wasn't even what caught him off guard so much. Conner ran his hands through his hair, staring up at the ceiling from his bed. He had never had such an instant reaction to a woman before. Adrienne Jeffries had affected him on every level.

She was five feet four of pure dynamite, it seemed. Conner normally preferred taller, more athletically built women—and with long blond hair. Adrienne Jeffries was slender, but short, and her hair definitely wasn't long and blond. Rather pixie-short and brown, with little chunks of copper in it. But Conner found his fingers itching to run through it.

He knew his behavior earlier today had been unprofessional and may have seemed borderline psychotic to Adrienne. Harrington had let Conner have it more than once on their way back to San Francisco from Lodi. Conner knew, whatever he was feeling, he had to get it under control before he saw her again in just a few short hours.

No matter what confusion Conner may have over his attraction to Adrienne, he had no confusion over his feelings about her so-called "abilities." Obviously years ago she had somehow convinced the Bureau she could track criminals like some supersleuth. Conner had no reason to believe she could do all that the FBI urban legends about her suggested she could do.

As far as he was concerned, she would come in, they would get all the insight from her that they could—if any—and then they would send her on her way. It shouldn't take more than a day. His boss would be appeased, and he and Harrington could get on with real law enforcement work and catch Simon Says as soon as possible.

And maybe, after Simon Says was apprehended, Conner would head back out to a certain horse ranch in Lodi and see Adrienne Jeffries again under very different circumstances.

But until then, Adrienne—and her abilities—were just a distraction. Something to draw his focus away from what he knew needed to be done to catch the killer. Conner couldn't allow that to happen. No matter how much he may want it to.

Conner decided to get up and get dressed since dawn was about to break anyway. He may as well go into the office and make an early start of what surely would be a long day. He wouldn't be surprised if Seth was there early, also.

FORTIFIED WITH MULTIPLE cups of coffee, Adrienne drove herself into San Francisco the next day. She needed the coffee after being awake most of the night—first packing and preparing for the trip, and then worrying about the toll it would take on her. The drive was relatively uneventful, but she found herself getting more and more uptight as she got closer to the city. Already she missed her little ranch and the serenity it offered.

And she hadn't even put herself in the clutches of the FBI yet.

She turned the radio up in her old Corolla as she crossed the Bay Bridge and entered the city. She forced herself to sing along to some familiar song by an '80s hair band. Singing helped her not to think too much and to ignore any buzzing she might start to hear in her head. With a population of nearly a million, Adrienne knew there would be people around the San Francisco area with malicious thoughts. There was nothing Adrienne could do about them, so she knew it was better to try not to hear them at all.

Adrienne navigated the hills and multiple one-way streets San Fran was famous for and finally parked at the FBI field office's parking garage. As she shut off her car, Adrienne braced herself to be bombarded by other people's thoughts in her head or to at least hear a dull roar of competing voices. She was pleasantly surprised to find just the slightest buzz—almost nothing.

Adrienne smiled. Evidently everybody in San Francisco must be having a good day or something. She didn't mind, less of a headache—literally—for her.

Upon entering the building, she was escorted up to the Violent Criminal Apprehension Program offices. She saw Conner Perigo as soon as she entered the main area. Dammit. The man looked just as good as he had yesterday. She had hoped she had imagined the thick black hair and gorgeous green eyes. But evidently not.

Those green eyes were fixed on her as Agent Perigo's partner, Seth, came over to meet her in the doorway.

"Ms. Jeffries, we're so glad you made it," Seth said as he led her over to an interrogation room. The two agents sat in the pair of seats on one side of the table and motioned for her to sit in a chair across from them.

Teams had obviously been drawn, and she wasn't on theirs.

"Not that I had much choice," Adrienne muttered. "But it's still okay to call me Adrienne."

She could feel Conner Perigo's eyes on her. Adrienne resisted the urge to fidget in her chair.

Agent Harrington smiled. "That's good. Please, like I said yesterday, call me Seth." He pointed at Agent Perigo. "And you can call him Conner. He promises to be on his best behavior today."

Somehow Adrienne doubted it.

"Okay, Seth, Conner it is, then." Adrienne decided she should try to make the best of the situation—not antagonize the agents, especially Conner. "But before we get started, I want your assurances that all charges or warrants or whatever against Rick Vincent will be dropped once I help you."

Conner spoke to her for the first time. "That won't be a problem, Adrienne. Neither of us were thrilled with how that went down."

Adrienne looked at Conner, and he nodded. She believed him. Whoever's idea it had been to use Vince as leverage, it definitely hadn't been Conner's. But that still didn't mean he liked or trusted her.

"Okay, Adrienne," Seth said. "We'd like to get started right away. But to be honest, we're not exactly sure how to proceed. Maybe you can provide us a little insight."

Adrienne took a deep breath. Might as well just get this over with. She had already made sure her purse contained a full bottle of ibuprofen. She would need most of it over the next few days.

"What can you tell me about the case?"

She watched as Conner and Seth—now in full FBI agent mode—looked at one another. Obviously until she proved herself and her abilities, they were loath to provide her with too much information.

"We have a serial killer on our hands. The victims are all women—five in the past ten months," Conner told her.

Adrienne waited to see if there would be further information, but evidently that was all they felt comfortable sharing with her.

"Okay, well, do you have anything from the crime scenes? Particularly anything the killer may have touched."

Seth responded this time. "There was no forensic evidence found at any of the scenes. Whoever the killer is, he's very careful."

No forensic evidence made it more difficult for Adrienne to get any sort of clear bearings about the killer, but not impossible.

"Do you have anything the killer might have touched, even with gloves on?"

Conner and Seth looked at each other once again. She saw Conner give a slight negative shake of his head.

Seth handed her an envelope that had been lying on the table. "We have some pictures of the crime scene. Will that help?"

Adrienne nodded and took the pictures. She braced herself as she opened the envelope. Death scenes were always jarring. She took out the first set of pictures, slowly looking at each one. The dead woman in the picture had been left in what looked like an abandoned warehouse of some sort. Multiple stab wounds covered her body. Different pictures showed the poor woman at various angles.

Three or four pictures in, Adrienne realized that, while she was horrified at what she was seeing, none of it was causing her any pain. Which was great, except for the fact that she also was not getting any insights or feelings from the pictures whatsoever.

Adrienne went through the entire set of crime scene photos for the woman in the warehouse. She then looked through them all again to be sure.

She felt nothing.

Adrienne looked up to find Conner and Seth watching her intently. She didn't know what to say—nothing like this had happened before when she had helped the FBI in the past. What was wrong with her?

"Do you have pictures of any of the other cases?" Adrienne finally asked.

"Yes. The ones you were just looking at is the first victim," Conner replied as Seth got out another set to show her.

First victim. Adrienne relaxed for a moment. Maybe

the reason she couldn't get any feelings from those pictures was because of the length of time that had passed between then and now. That had never happened to her before, but it seemed plausible.

Adrienne tried to clear all thoughts from her head as she took the next set of photos. Another stabbing scene with a young woman. This time it seemed she had been left under a highway overpass bridge.

Again Adrienne was horrified by the violence but felt nothing in terms of the killer's thoughts, plans or motivations.

This continued for the next hour as Adrienne pored over the photos again and again. Nothing. Her insight wasn't working at all. Although the agents across from her never said anything, she could tell their frustration was growing.

"I'm sorry," Adrienne said, handing the photos back across the table. "I'm not getting anything from any of these."

Conner Perigo didn't look a bit surprised. "Do pictures not work for you?"

"They did in the past. The glimpses I would get from crime scene photos weren't as clear as actually being at the crime scene or touching something the perpetrator touched, but there was always something."

"I see." Perigo's smug tone grated on Adrienne's nerves. Obviously her lack of ability to perform here was just confirming what he had suspected all along— she was a fake.

Adrienne sat back in her chair and rubbed her eyes with both hands. On one hand she was happy her gifts weren't working—it definitely saved her a literal headache—but on the other hand she desperately wanted to show Conner Perigo he was wrong.

Adrienne crossed her arms on the table and laid her forehead on her arms, taking a few deep breaths. She needed to center herself. She needed to block out all the buzzing around her and focus.

That's when Adrienne realized there was no buzzing going on inside her head at all. It was completely silent.

Even if she wasn't getting any reading from the pictures, she should still be hearing some sort of low murmur just by the very nature of being in a large building filled with people. Everyone gave off static. The more people around, the louder it was to her. That was why she chose to live in a relatively isolated area—so she wouldn't have to put up with the white noise all the time.

As long as there was no one with malice in their thoughts, then everything stayed at a low static— annoying, but bearable. But sinister intent would instantly throw pictures into Adrienne's mind. Along with searing pain. When she touched something that had been handled by someone malicious, she also could usually get some sort of picture of what had been going through the mind of that person.

She should have been able to do that with the crime scene photos, but she couldn't. Right now not only was she not getting any pictures in her head, she wasn't even getting any static. That had never happened before.

The silence was so unusual to her it was eerie. But not unwelcome.

She had no idea how long the silence would last. But the way the agents across the table were looking at her—especially Conner—they were not willing to wait long to see. Maybe she would get out of this after all. But then she thought of Vince back at the ranch. She wanted to get rid of whatever guillotine blade that the FBI had hanging over him.

If only for Vince's sake, she wanted her gifts to work, just this one time. Although, if she were honest, Adrienne knew she also wanted to show Conner Perigo what she was capable of.

She watched Conner and Seth look at each other. Seth finally broke the awkward silence that had been building. "Look, it's early. Maybe I can get you a cup of coffee or something and that will help."

Adrienne nodded, grateful for the reprieve. "Yeah, coffee would be great. I didn't get a whole lot of sleep last night. I'm not sure exactly what's going on. Maybe I've just been out of the game for a little too long and need to ease my way back in."

"No problem," Seth said. "You stay here and look through the pictures a little more. Conner will stay, too. I'll get coffee and be back soon. Anything in particular in it?"

"No, just black, thanks."

Seth stood. "I'll run down to the coffee shop in the lobby and get it. If you drink what's in our office, you're liable to have to be chained up in the next full moon."

Conner looked over at Seth. "If you're going down there, I'll have the usual."

Seth rolled his eyes and snickered, walking out the door without responding.

"What's 'the usual'?" Adrienne asked Conner, her curiosity piqued by Seth's response. In the long silence that followed, Adrienne wasn't sure he was going to tell her.

"Skinny vanilla chai tea latte with no foam and sugar-free vanilla," Conner finally said. "I get ragged pretty hard from the guys."

Adrienne couldn't help it; she broke out into a smile. The thought of this big tough-looking agent whose shirt seemed to be perpetually slightly wrinkled and whose tie was probably one of a dozen stuffed in his glove compartment, using the words *skinny* and *latte* when referring to his coffee was downright hilarious.

Conner smiled back, looking sheepish. "I know. It doesn't exactly fit the tough-guy image."

The way he cocked his head to the side caused his black hair to fall onto his forehead. Before she could stop herself, Adrienne's fingers reached up to tuck the hair into place. Halfway to his head she realized what she was about to do and immediately lowered her hand back to the table. She studied the photos again intently, hoping he hadn't noticed her...

Her *what?* Desire to touch him? Inexplicable need to be closer to him? Complete lack of control of her own hands?

Adrienne stared down at the pictures for a long time without looking up, grateful for the distraction, although she still wasn't getting any helpful info from them.

"Are you sure these are all the work of the same killer?" she finally asked.

"Yes." There was no doubt in Conner's voice. "He has a signature that makes it clear they are all the same killer." He didn't offer any information about what that signature was. Adrienne didn't ask, knowing he wouldn't tell her anyway.

Adrienne was tired of looking at these poor dead women. It was so frustrating to review them without any understanding as to what and how it had happened. She pushed the pictures back toward Conner's side of the table.

"I need a break. I can't look at them anymore right now."

She gazed at Conner, expecting to find more of

yesterday's hostile and condescending tone from him. Instead, he looked attentive, even the slightest bit sympathetic.

"You know, it's okay," Conner said gently. "Whatever's going on here, whatever reason you're not able to help us, it really is okay."

Adrienne couldn't help but respond to his gentleness. "This has never happened to me. The…nothing. I've always been able to hear or see or feel *something* before."

"It's been a long time since you've done anything like this, right? Maybe you just need to ease yourself back into it, like you said." The gentleness was still there but Adrienne could hear the disbelief that colored his tone.

"You don't understand. I always hear something when I'm around people, no matter what. It's like a buzz. But right now I don't hear anything."

"Maybe it's the pressure of the situation. Or maybe the pictures are too old or something."

"Yeah, maybe."

"Look, Adrienne. I want to give you this chance, while we're here alone, to tell me if there's something you want to tell me. You know, about your abilities or about when you worked for the FBI before."

"I don't understand." Adrienne was honestly puzzled.

"I mean, if you were in some way exaggerating what you could do—in terms of profiling and working for the FBI—either then or now. Or, hell, even if you had completely tricked the Bureau before, you can tell me, and I'll make sure nothing happens to you."

"What?"

"I'm just telling you, I'll protect you from any repercussions. We'll come up with some reason why you can't help us that everyone will buy. I'll even make sure Rick Vincent is taken care of and won't be arrested."

He had the nerve to sit there with his gorgeous green eyes and say this to her.

Adrienne struggled to keep her temper from boiling over. "So let me make sure I understand this. You think I deceived the FBI ten years ago when I worked for them and that I'm back again, lying now. Wasting my time and yours."

She could see Conner attempting damage control in his mind. But she never gave him a chance to speak.

"And you, very magnanimously I might add, are offering to protect me if I just come clean now and, what, admit this was all a hoax?"

"Adrienne, calm down."

Adrienne raised her eyebrows at that—no man should ever tell an upset woman to *calm down*—but she kept quiet.

"I'm just trying to offer you an out if you need it."

"Well, thank you, Agent Perigo." She saw him grimace. "But despite you thinking I'm a liar and a cheat, not to mention some sort of juvenile attention-seeker, I don't need an out!"

"Listen, I'm not trying to offend you. But I've been an agent a long time, and I've never seen anything that suggested a gift such as yours is real. As a matter of fact, the exact opposite is true. When someone comes forth and claims to be 'psychic' and know something about a case, almost always he or she is involved in some way."

Adrienne took a deep breath. Conner was skeptical. She had dealt with skepticism before, even considered it healthy. No one should blindly believe someone else without reason. Why did she feel the need to prove herself to him when she never had felt that way about anyone else?

"I'm not a psychic," Adrienne said quietly.

"Whatever you want to call it. Good, smart detective work is what solves cases, not hocus-pocus."

"It's not magic, Perigo. It's just the way my brain works. Some people are geniuses with musical instruments. Some are whizzes when it comes to math. My brain is just wired differently than most people."

"Then why isn't your gift working now?"

Temper threatened again. "I don't know!"

Seth chose that moment to come in with the coffee. He put the cup carrier down, looking back and forth between Adrienne and Conner, noticing the obvious tension between them.

"Here you go, Adrienne. Coffee, black. And here's your froufrou, princess," he said as he handed Conner his drink. "You owe me $4.50."

"How come I have to pay, but she doesn't?"

"Because her drink didn't involve an embarrassing list of words to order." Seth sat down in his chair. "Anything come to you while I was gone?"

"Nothing, Seth, I'm sorry."

"Don't worry, we've got time."

Adrienne hoped time would help.

Chapter Five

Six hours later Adrienne still had not experienced anything helpful to the case. Conner and Seth had left her alone in the interrogation room but stood just a few feet away on the other side of two-way glass. They could see Adrienne, but she couldn't see them.

All day Conner had watched Adrienne pore over the pictures again and again. He had watched her try different methods, studying each picture one at time, spreading as many out on the table as could fit, flipping through them all quickly. Everything she tried ended with that same blended look of frustration and confusion.

He had to give it to her; if she was pulling some sort of scam, she was definitely tenacious about it.

They hadn't talked again about his get-out-of-jail-free offer. She seemed legitimately offended by it, so he didn't bring it back up. Conner shrugged. He was just trying to provide her an escape if she needed it—not all those things she had accused him of doing.

He and Seth had tried to help her any way they could. They encouraged her to take breaks, walked her outside to get fresh air and took her on a lengthy lunch to get her away from all of it for a while. Nothing seemed to help. Now, watching her, she just looked exhausted.

Conner would be angry at Adrienne, but Adrienne was so frustrated with herself that he couldn't bring himself to be mad. But he was definitely concerned that they had wasted an entire day doing something that had provided zero results. Conner had stayed with her the whole day—he could admit it was at least partially because he didn't trust her out of his sight—and watched her get more frustrated and disheartened as the day went along.

"I guess this is a bust, huh?" Seth broke into Conner's thoughts as they both watched Adrienne. "Looks like you were right."

"About what?" Conner asked, breaking his gaze from Adrienne to look at his partner.

"That this was all bogus and a waste of time. She's done nothing to help us."

"Yeah, I guess, but you definitely can't say she didn't try. I almost want her to get a feeling or reading or whatever, just so she won't have that look on her face anymore."

"Yeah, she looks pretty upset. I told Chief Kelly that we weren't having much luck with her. He wanted to know if we thought she was withholding information on purpose."

Conner shook his head. "I don't think so. If she is, she's one hell of an actress. What do you think?"

Seth gazed through the two-way glass again. "Who knows? But it doesn't seem like she found something and isn't telling. The chief wanted to know if we wanted him to come in and talk to her since she had worked with him before. I told him no. That okay?"

"Yeah. The way she spoke about Chief Kelly before,

I don't think seeing him would help any. What are we supposed to do? Call her a failure and send her home?" Conner asked.

"The chief wants us to consider letting her see the packages Simon Says sent. The hair locks."

Conner's eyebrows shot up. "I'm not ready to do that yet. I don't want to give away anything that detailed about the case."

"I told the chief that. Bureau's going to pay to put her up in a hotel room at least for tonight. See where we are by the end of tomorrow. Maybe she just needs a good night's sleep."

"All right. But look at her, she's exhausted. How about I'll drive with her in her car to the hotel, and you follow and give me a ride back."

Seth nodded and headed out of the door. "Sure. Let me shut down my computer, and I'll be ready to go. I'll meet you at her hotel."

Conner walked over to the interrogation room. Adrienne was still poring over the pictures. She didn't even look up when he entered.

"Hey, you about ready to call it a day?" Conner asked as he sat down across from her.

"Conner, I still don't have anything. *Nothing.* These women…they died so horribly, and I can't seem to help them in any way."

"Well, if it helps, Seth and I have been feeling that exact same frustration for weeks."

Adrienne shook her head. "I don't know how you do it."

"You just do the best you can with what you have."

"Well, right now, it looks like I have absolutely nothing."

Conner reached over and took the pictures from her.

"That's enough for the day. You need a break. We're going to put you up at a hotel, and we'll start fresh in the morning after a good night's sleep."

As Conner put each of the pictures back in their respective envelopes, he watched Adrienne put her elbows on the table and rest her head in her hands. She looked fragile, breakable. Conner was overwhelmed by the urge to protect her.

And kiss her.

Of course that still didn't mean he trusted her or believed what she said she could do.

When he finished putting away the photos, Adrienne stood with him. He held the door open for her as they walked into the hallway. His other hand hovered near the small of her back.

"I'm going to drive you in your car to the hotel. Seth will pick me up and bring me back here."

"I'm okay to drive," Adrienne insisted, stopping.

"I know you'd probably be fine, but San Fran streets can be crazy even for those of us who drive them every day. Just let me do this for you, okay?"

She looked at him for a long moment.

"What?" Conner finally asked.

"You're kind of being nice to me. Not sure what to do with that."

Conner wanted to reach out and stroke her cheek but, instead, squeezed her shoulder in a friendly manner. "Well, how about I'll go back to being mean to you tomorrow? After we both get some sleep."

Her smiled transfixed her whole face—an impish grin that suited her features perfectly. It took Conner's breath away. And definitely brought back the urge to kiss her.

She stuck out her hand, and they shook on it. "Okay, a truce, then. At least for today."

Conner tried to find a neutral topic as they headed to her car in the parking garage. "Neutral" wasn't exactly simple for them, considering they couldn't talk about his work or her work or his background or her background or the city, or most other topics lest it bring them back to why they were here.

"We've had some really great weather here lately," Conner finally said.

Adrienne looked at him as if he were crazy. It was San Francisco. The weather here rarely strayed from the averages.

Conner shrugged and grinned. "Just trying to make conversation that doesn't break the truce."

"You don't have to pander to me, Perigo. I don't mind you being skeptical about what I can do. It's your petty comments I can live without."

All five foot four of her was glaring up at him. He swallowed the laughter he knew would just get him in more trouble.

"Yes, ma'am."

"How long have you worked for the Bureau?" Adrienne asked as they entered the garage. Adrienne directed them to her car, and Conner opened her door for her.

"Twelve years. I was at Quantico for about four years, as part of CIRG—Critical Incident Response Group. I liked that and kind of naturally morphed into ViCAP."

Adrienne rolled her eyes. "The FBI loves its acronyms. So how did you end up out here from Virginia?"

"Natural progression, mostly. My family is all on the

West Coast. My grandmother lived here in San Francisco, and I stayed with her for a while when a ViCAP position opened. Worked out for everyone."

As they drove, Conner answered Adrienne's questions about his time at the FBI. He had arrived at the San Francisco office not long after she had left eight years ago but had always been in a different section of the Bureau office. If she had stayed just a year longer, they might have crossed paths.

Conner parked the car at the hotel and got Adrienne's bag out of the trunk and walked her into the lobby, allowing her to get checked in.

She turned and offered her hand for him to shake and to take her bag. "Thanks for getting me here, Conner. I guess we'll just pick up tomorrow?"

Conner found he wasn't ready to let her go just yet. He took her outstretched hand, but turned it in his palm. "I'll walk you to your room. That okay?"

Adrienne gave him a shy smile and pulled her hand away. "Sure. Thanks."

They strolled to the elevator and went up to her floor. At her room's door she slid by him and opened it with her key card.

They walked in, and Conner placed her bag on the bed. Out of habit he checked the closet and bathroom to make sure both were empty. When he came back into the room, Adrienne stood looking at him with an eyebrow raised. "Everything clear?"

"Sorry—habit. Look, before I go, let me give you my number, just in case you need anything."

Adrienne tried to find a pen and paper so he could write it down but didn't see any. She tossed him her phone. "Just program it straight in."

Conner punched in his number and handed it back to her. "I guess I'll see you in the morning. I'll come by and get you around nine o'clock?"

"Sure."

Conner watched as a pinched look came over her face, and Adrienne's gaze dropped to the ground. "Listen, I just want to say I'm sorry I was so useless today. I'm sure tomorrow will be better. It has to be."

Conner put a finger under her chin, tilting her head up. "Hey, you tried your best. That's all anybody could ask."

"Yeah? Well, my best didn't accomplish squat today." Frustration fairly oozed out of her.

"I've certainly had those types of days myself. You just have to recalibrate yourself for tomorrow."

Adrienne nodded. That she seemed to understand. "Thanks, Conner." She smiled softly.

That soft smile was his undoing. Almost without meaning to, he bent down and kissed her. He meant the kiss to be brief, comforting. Conner was surprised when Adrienne, in turn, deepened the kiss. He felt her hands grab the lapel of his jacket and pull him closer, and she stood up on tiptoe.

Conner's armed snaked around her waist as her mouth opened and her tongue ran along his lips. He was pulling her even closer when a brisk knock came from the door that wasn't completely closed. They shot apart as Seth walked in.

"Hey, Conner, you ready?" Seth looked from Adrienne to Conner and recognition flared in his eyes. "Oh, sorry. I'm leaving now."

"No, hang on, Seth. I'm coming." Conner looked at Adrienne, who seemed as shaken up as he felt. "I'll see you in the morning, okay? We'll start completely over with everything."

Adrienne smiled. "Fresh start sounds good. With everything."

THE FIRST THOUGHT that invaded Adrienne's consciousness when she awoke the next morning was that the static was back. She sat up in her hotel bed, holding herself still to be sure. Yes, it was definitely back—the buzz she got from being around people. Adrienne grinned. It was annoying, but she was thrilled.

Another noise joined the slight static—her stomach growling. She was starving. Last night she had had no interest in food. The combination of the day she had had and the sleepless night before had caught up with her. All she had wanted to do was curl up and go to sleep, even though it had been early in the evening.

Once Conner had left, Adrienne had taken a shower trying to wash away the pictures of those women—all dead—and her failure to help them. After she had dried off, she had grabbed an oversize T-shirt out of her suitcase and had fallen into bed, asleep as soon as her head hit the pillow.

Now it was early in the morning; the sun was barely up. Adrienne wandered into the bathroom and began brushing her teeth. She didn't mind waking up at an hour beginning with five. Living on a ranch had turned her into an early riser.

She brushed her hair and picked some clothes out of her suitcase. She put on khaki pants and a blue button-down blouse. The rest of her clothes she hung in the closet or put in a drawer; the slight buzzing sound in her head hopefully meant she would be staying longer, able to help Conner and Seth find the killer of those women.

Adrienne wasn't sure exactly when she had completely committed herself to helping the FBI. But she knew it was sometime yesterday when she had looked through all those pictures of the murdered women, helpless to do anything. Conner and Seth sitting across from her, hopeful she could provide information that would give them a lead, and her able to do nothing. She had always considered her gift a nuisance at the very best, and often downright painful and debilitating; but yesterday, when she couldn't use it, she knew she wanted it back.

And now it looked like it was.

A few minutes later Adrienne was ready to leave the hotel. It was still too early to meet Conner and head to the Bureau's office. She decided she would spend an hour or so at a local coffee shop within walking distance, then would call Conner and tell him that she would meet him at the field office earlier than 9:00 a.m. She wanted to be there as early as possible so she could get a look at those pictures again. Provide some sort of insight and hopefully help crack open the case.

Adrienne knew she also wanted to see Conner's face when she was able to provide intel he totally wasn't expecting. Certainly Conner had become more kind as yesterday had progressed, and that kiss had been unexpected and magical. But Adrienne knew Conner still didn't believe her or trust her.

Adrienne smiled. For once she was almost looking forward to the physical discomfort that came from using her gift. It would be worth it.

Adrienne walked up one of San Francisco's famous hills to get to the nearest coffee shop. She breathed in the crisp morning air, grateful for exercise and being outside, however briefly. She knew today was going to be another long day.

Adrienne entered the coffee shop, surprised at the number of people already there, despite the early hour. The static inside her mind became quite a bit louder. Adrienne got in line, hoping a cup of coffee would ward off the headache forming.

She smiled, thinking of Conner's froufrou drink order. Skinny vanilla chai latte… Adrienne couldn't even remember the rest.

After ordering and paying for her drink, Adrienne made her way over to one of the few empty tables by the window. She was a step away from a chair when the screaming began in her head. The sound was deafening, as if someone had put headphones over her ears, then turned up the volume as loud as possible. The pain immediately blinded her and she stumbled toward the table, blindly grasping for its edge with her free hand. She tumbled into the seat trying to keep hold of her consciousness.

I will kill her! I will kill them both!

The general rage clouded everything, but that one thought filtered through her mind over and over.

She was crushing the foam cup of coffee still clutched in her hand. The scalding liquid spilled out, but she couldn't force her muscles to relax their locked grip of the cup. She felt the burn almost distantly, secondary to the pain in her head that seemed to shoot daggers into her eyes.

I will kill them both!

The scream was getting louder now, and closer. Adrienne forced her eyes to open slightly, although the agony from the effort nearly caused her to black out.

She looked around the coffee shop trying to find the two people the screaming voice referred to. She spotted them in the opposite corner—a man and woman, both in their mid-twenties, huddled close together. Their hands were linked, and they smiled and spoke softly to one another.

There was no doubt this was who the voice was referring to. Adrienne had no idea how far the man with the voice was from the coffee shop. She could see him storming up a hill—his anger growing with every step—but she couldn't tell how far he was. Given the loudness of his thoughts, Adrienne didn't think it would be very long before he arrived.

And when he did, the young couple would die.

Suddenly the volume of the enraged man lowered, and Adrienne could see him walking in through a double set of doors in a coffeehouse. Adrienne whirled her head around to see if it was this one he was entering and wilted back into her chair in relief when she saw it wasn't.

He was in another location of this same chain, somewhere nearby. But there was one on every corner, so she had no idea how far away he was. His screaming thoughts had subsided a bit as he concentrated on looking for the couple, not yet knowing he was in the wrong shop.

Adrienne knew she had to act now. Whether the enraged man found the correct coffee shop in a few moments or twenty minutes, he would still eventually find it. She had to get help and warn the couple.

She forced herself to loosen the grip on the ruined coffee cup and reached into her purse for her phone. She stared at it in her hand for a long moment, trying to decide what she would say to 9-1-1 when she called. She wasn't sure she could get out a coherent sentence. Then she remembered Conner had programmed his number into her phone last night. He may not trust her, but he would at least not ignore her.

She pressed Send on her phone, praying his was still the last number called, knowing that looking through a contact list now would be impossible. His sleepy voice answered on the second ring.

"Hello?"

"Conner." The one word was all she could manage. Her voice was weak and shaky.

"Adrienne? What's wrong? Are you okay?"

"I need help." Her voice was barely more than a whisper now.

"Where are you? At the hotel?"

"No. I'm at the coffee shop. Up the hill." She took a breath between each sentence. The white dots were floating in front of her eyes now, but she fought to hold on to consciousness.

"Okay. Hang on for just a second." She could hear him saying something to someone else. She leaned her head against the cool glass of the wall next to her table.

"Adrienne? Listen, Seth is already near the office, he should be there in five minutes. I'm on my way, too. Should I call 9-1-1?" The urgency in Conner's voice made it through to her subconscious. He believed her that something was wrong; she felt profound relief.

"Conner..." she started weakly.

"Yes? What is it?"

"Hurry. He's going to kill..." Adrienne was unable to finish the sentence. The man's voice screaming inside her head hit her so hard that the phone flew out of her hand as she brought her hands up to keep her skull from splitting.

He was looking for them again, the intent to kill at the forefront on his mind, rage that he couldn't find them a close second. And he was getting nearer.

Adrienne knew Conner had Seth coming to help her, but even five minutes would be too late. She had to warn the couple sitting across the coffee shop. Get them to leave. Bar the door. Do *something*.

Or people would die.

Adrienne attempted to stand up, but her legs wouldn't seem to support her. She took her hands from her head and put them on the table to use as leverage to get up, vaguely aware of the concerned looks she was getting from the people around her.

I will kill them both!

The pain seared through her head with each of his thoughts. His feelings were beyond just a jealous rage. It was a malicious desire to see them both suffer, to watch them cower in fear. And he didn't care if he had to kill others to achieve that goal.

Adrienne finally hoisted herself up from her seat, leaning heavily against the table. She looked down and saw a drop of blood on the table and realized her nose must be bleeding. She wiped it with the back of her hand as she took her first unsteady steps toward the couple in the corner across the way.

The trip seemed to take forever. Adrienne concentrated on putting one foot in front of the other. She was losing her peripheral vision, could feel blackness closing in around her, but fought it back. He was getting closer, Adrienne knew.

She finally reached the table where the couple sat, still gazing at each other, oblivious to Adrienne's agony.

They looked up in alarm when she finally stumbled into their table.

"Excuse me…" the boyfriend started in a perturbed tone.

"Oh, my gosh, are you all right? Your nose is bleeding," the woman asked. Both she and the boyfriend stood to help steady Adrienne.

Adrienne couldn't think straight. How could she get them to leave?

"A man," she finally said, her breath sawing in and out of her chest as if she were running a marathon. "Coming. Hurt you."

Adrienne could tell they didn't understand, had no idea of the danger they were in. She knew they were out of time, could feel the man getting closer. What could she do? She had to make them leave. Maybe if she could just get the woman out.

Adrienne turned to the younger woman and grabbed her upper arms, trying to keep herself upright. She took a deep breath and focused desperately on the words she needed to say.

"Can you, please." *Breathe.* "Go get me." *Breathe.* "A wet paper towel." *Breathe.* "From bathroom."

The woman looked very confused, but finally nodded. "Sure. Just hang on. Do we need to call a doctor?"

"No, not yet," Adrienne answered. She slid into the woman's vacated chair with relief as Adrienne watched her cross to the bathroom. Hopefully it would be enough.

The boyfriend looked at Adrienne with a blend of concern and apprehension. Adrienne didn't blame him for either.

The door slammed open behind her. He never said

a word, but at this close proximity, Adrienne could see every malicious thought the man had. He was sure they were here. He looked around at all the tables and eventually got to where Adrienne and the boyfriend were sitting. He didn't even pause to glance twice at them. The woman he searched for was not there; Adrienne had sent her to the bathroom.

A rage overwhelmed the man once again that he had not found his prey. Adrienne whimpered, the pain consuming her, but nobody heard. The man turned to walk back out the door.

"Here, miss, is this enough? Your nose is bleeding more." The woman rushed across the coffee shop with paper towels in her hands.

Adrienne felt the absolute glee the man experienced when he heard the woman's voice. He would not be denied his vengeance after all.

He was only a few feet behind where Adrienne sat. Adrienne knew he was about to reach for the gun he had hidden in his pocket. Using the remainder of her strength, she got out of the chair and hefted herself toward the man, knocking into him. He pushed her off easily and Adrienne slid to the floor.

By now the woman had recognized the enraged man, and was pulling her lover away and around the back of the coffee bar. The man began to draw his gun out of his pocket. Adrienne tried to get up but couldn't make her body respond.

"Sir, I am an agent for the Federal Bureau of Investigation." A voice rang out from near the back door. "I need you to lay down your weapon and put your hands on your head." It was Seth Harrington. Conner had gotten him here in time.

Adrienne felt the rage briefly overtake the man

before he resigned himself to the fact that he had been caught. Sirens could be heard pulling up outside the coffee shop. The man slowly put the gun on the ground and his hands behind his head.

Over the next few minutes, organized panic ensued. Uniformed officers filed into the coffee shop, taking statements and making sure no one was hurt. Someone helped Adrienne up into a chair since she was still unsteady on her feet. The attacker was handcuffed and placed in the back of squad car just outside the door.

Although he was no longer in the coffee shop, his proximity, combined with his continued malevolence, continued to cause jagged pains to shoot through Adrienne's head. She could still hear everything he would've done to them if he had just been given the chance. She could feel bile pooling in her stomach, and she wasn't sure how much longer she could hold on.

Adrienne stood, prepared to stumble her way to the bathroom if she was going to lose the contents of her stomach, when all of a sudden the pain and noise in her head completely stopped.

Caught off guard by the blessed silence, Adrienne looked around in confusion. Then she saw him.

Conner.

He had pulled up in his vehicle, double-parked and was rushing inside. Straight toward her. She could see myriad emotions crossing his face: confusion, concern, relief. He didn't stop until he was standing right in front of her.

"Conner..." Adrienne reached for him and found she couldn't hold on any longer.

Her last thought was hoping Conner would catch her, then she slipped unconscious to the floor.

Chapter Six

Conner caught Adrienne as she dropped to the floor, unconscious.

As he had pulled up in his vehicle—he didn't even want to think of all the traffic laws he had broken getting here from his house in record time—he had seen Adrienne inside the coffee shop. At first he was overwhelmed with relief just to see she was okay. But as he had rushed closer to Adrienne, he had realized she definitely was not okay.

There was zero color in her face, except for the dried blood that had trickled from her nose. Against her unnatural paleness, the blood stood out with jarring brightness. She was on her feet but looked none too steady. As he came through the door, some sort of shocked look passed over her features; she took a step toward him and said his name.

Then promptly collapsed.

Conner grabbed her as she fell and gently lowered her to the ground. "Seth!" he yelled out to his partner, who was talking to a witness over by the coffee bar. "I need help here."

When Seth saw Conner holding Adrienne, he quickly made his way to them.

"Is she okay? What happened?"

"I wanted to ask you that. I walked in and basically caught her as she collapsed." Conner brushed a stray strand of hair that had fallen onto her forehead. Adrienne sighed and moved a little toward his hand. Although her movement reassured Conner, the absolute lack of color in her face did not. "Did the perp hurt her?"

"There were no reports of him doing anything. He was pulling the gun as I walked in. Didn't resist arrest or put up any fight." Seth shrugged.

"So what happened to her?"

"I don't know. She was sitting on the ground when I got here but then was at the table when I looked over at her again. She didn't seem hurt."

Conner didn't like it. "Why is her nose bleeding? Did she get hit?" He couldn't see any bruising or swelling around her face, so couldn't figure out what the blood was from.

"Not from any reports I've gotten. As a matter of fact, the only one who seemed to be acting odd—before the perp pulled the gun, that is—was Adrienne. More than one person has said she looked sick or drunk or something."

Conner looked down at the woman lying against his arm. She was stirring more, and he knew she would be regaining consciousness soon. "Did you talk to her at all?"

"No. I was too busy making sure our psycho wouldn't open fire on anyone."

Conner felt more movement from Adrienne and watched as her beautiful hazel eyes opened. She looked at him with confusion.

"Hey." He smiled at her gently. "Don't try to move too much. You passed out."

Adrienne brought a hand up to her head. "The man was going to attack the woman."

"I don't know exactly what was going to happen, but Seth stopped him. He's been taken into custody."

Adrienne nodded. "Good. That's good. Can you help me up?"

Conner noticed some of the color was returning to her face. That was a good sign. He and Seth reached down on either side of her to get her into the chair a few feet away.

"What happened to you?" Conner asked as she sat down. "Did you get hit or something? You have dried blood under your nose."

Adrienne brought her hand self-consciously to her face. "No. Sometimes that just happens. I'm okay."

Conner noticed the raised red marks on her wrist. He took her hand away from her face to look at it more closely. Her entire hand was covered by the angry welts, and on some parts there was even blistering.

"What the hell happened to your hand?" Conner asked, careful not to touch what were obviously burns.

Adrienne looked down at her arm and hand. "I think I spilled my coffee on myself."

"Doesn't it hurt?"

Adrienne nodded. "Yes. But up until a few minutes ago, my head hurt much worse, and I kind of forgot about my hand."

Seth whistled through his teeth. "I'll get you a cold compress to put on it."

Conner looked at her hand, then her face. "I should take you to the hospital."

"No!" Adrienne's response was vehement. "I'm okay.

It hurts, but putting something cold on it will help. I don't need a hospital. I promise."

Conner was torn but decided not to push it. The burns, although painful-looking, were mostly first degree. Even the blisters were clear, suggesting superficial scalding—not anything that would require prolonged medical attention.

Seth returned in a moment with a bowl of water and a clean washcloth. He then excused himself to go help some uniformed officers finish up with the witnesses.

Conner took the washcloth and dipped it in the water. It was cold. "Do you mind if I help?"

Adrienne laid her arm out on the table between them. "Thanks."

She sucked in her breath as the wet cloth touched her skin—the water was chilled but not icy, helping to lessen the pain and cease any further burning.

"Sorry." Conner grimaced. "I know it has to hurt."

"No, the cold feels good. Thanks." She smiled at him, and Conner was glad to see even more of her color was coming back into her face. She looked almost normal.

"How did you spill your coffee?"

"I could…hear the man's thoughts and they…startled me."

Conner noticed her hesitations. Obviously she expected some sort of argument from him about her gifts.

To be honest he didn't know how he felt about her special skills. When he had gotten her phone call a little while ago, he could tell immediately that something was wrong. Dangerously wrong.

As soon as she had said she needed help, he had gotten Seth on the other line. Conner hadn't questioned, hadn't hesitated—just knew she needed him and had responded.

He could admit to himself that his instantaneous response in coming to her aid without knowing details was pretty odd behavior, especially since he had all but called her a phony and a liar over the past couple of days.

But he had known—*known*—when she had called today that the situation was dire from the very beginning. She had needed him to help her, but he couldn't get there quickly enough, so he had sent Seth, who had been closer.

And thank God, if the perp had been drawing a weapon when Seth had arrived.

Conner took the washcloth gently away from Adrienne's hand and wrist, and dipped it in the cold water again. Wringing it out, he placed it back on her arm.

"So you knew he was going to kill her?" Conner asked.

"Yes. That's what I was certain about most of all. He was definitely planning to kill her and the man she was with."

Conner nodded but didn't say anything else. She had obviously been through a lot already today. He didn't want to say anything that would come across as combative.

"You could hear what he was thinking?"

Adrienne nodded gingerly. "It was like he was screaming his thoughts right in my ears. And I could see what he was seeing."

"You could actually see him?"

"Not see him, exactly. More like see things through his eyes."

Conner nodded to encourage her.

"I know he went into some other coffee shops looking for them before coming here."

Conner made a mental note to check into that. Maybe somebody would remember seeing the guy.

"When he couldn't find them," Adrienne continued, "he got more and more furious."

"When did you call me?"

"As soon as I realized he was going to make it here to this coffeehouse soon. I wasn't sure how long I had before he did, but I knew it wouldn't be very long."

She looked away, over toward the table where the couple had been sitting.

"I called you while the guy was having a momentarily sane period, when he walked into another coffeehouse. He had to put his rage and malice aside, and concentrate on seeing if she was there. That's what allowed me to pull it together long enough to call. I'm glad your number was in my phone, or I never would've gotten through to anyone."

"Why didn't you call 9-1-1?"

Adrienne gave a quiet bark of unamused laughter. "And told them what? That there was a man coming up the street, and I knew he planned to kill someone?"

No, that probably would not have gone over well with the 9-1-1 dispatcher. A city the size of San Francisco got a variety of prank calls every day. Even though they would've sent out a patrol unit as standard procedure, it would not have been a priority and wouldn't have been quick.

"Nine-one-one would still have sent a squad car. Or you could've lied and said he was already here."

Adrienne nodded. "Yeah, but I wasn't thinking too clearly at the time. Just trying to engage in normal functions, like breathing and staying upright, was taking all my concentration."

Conner remembered the terrified tenor of Adrienne's voice when she had called. The hesitation and breathlessness in how she'd talked. He realized now how difficult even their very short conversation had been for her.

"I'm glad you called me." Conner reached over and stroked her elbow far from the area affected by the burn.

Adrienne smiled tiredly at him. "I'm glad you believed me."

Conner shrugged. He wasn't sure he believed, exactly, but he had acted.

"Losing you in the middle of a sentence like that scared me. What happened?"

"The guy was furious when he realized the woman was not in the coffee shop down the block. He was so intent on hurting her—it was like a bomb went off in my head."

"Is that when your nose started bleeding?"

Adrienne brought a corner of the washcloth on her arm up to her nose, wiping the dried blood. "I guess so. I know that's when I decided I had to get over to the couple and try to get them out."

"So you went to talk to them?"

"Talk? I'm not sure that *talk* is the right word. I stumbled over to their table, literally. I couldn't figure out what to say—my brain felt like mush." Adrienne looked up at him with panic in her eyes. "Finally they noticed my nose was bleeding, and the lady got me a wet paper towel from the bathroom. She had just disappeared out of sight when the guy walked in."

Conner saw Adrienne shudder. Whatever she was remembering about this guy, she definitely didn't like it.

"I thought we were going to make it," Adrienne said

in a low voice. "But then she exited the bathroom, and he saw her."

Conner took the wet cloth off her arm again—the burn was looking better, although still angry—and waited for her to continue.

"I tried to get over to the guy to stop him myself. But his thoughts…" Adrienne closed her eyes. "They were so *loud*. So unbearably loud." She cringed again, and Conner found himself cringing with her.

"I tried to get to him, but he basically just brushed me off, and I fell and couldn't seem to get up even though I wasn't hurt. I didn't have any more strength." Adrienne looked at Conner with distress in her eyes. "I just knew he was going to kill them, Conner. I *knew* it."

"But he didn't," Conner reminded her.

"Thanks to Seth. He got here literally in the nick of time."

"You know, this is all going to be really iffy in court. His lawyer will argue the guy basically had a gun and made a bad judgment about when it was okay to take it out of his pocket. He didn't actually threaten anybody with it. We have no proof of any intent to harm the woman or the other man. At best the gunman will probably get charged with illegal possession of a firearm."

Adrienne nodded. "I know. I don't stand up well as a witness in court, I'm sure. But the important thing is, nobody was hurt today."

Conner gestured down at her burnt arm. "Not exactly."

"I'll be fine." Adrienne took the washcloth from him.

Conner took her hand in his. He rubbed his fingers gently on the part of her hand that wasn't burned. "I'm still sorry."

Adrienne smiled shyly, then withdrew her hand. Conner looked around him. Things were wrapping up. The man had already been taken away by the local police. Conner motioned to Seth, and Seth made his way over to them.

"Everything almost done here?" Conner asked him, standing up.

"Yeah. Seems like the perp was the ex-husband of the lady. Although they've been separated for over a year, he totally freaked out when he discovered she was dating someone else."

"He tell you that?" Conner asked.

"No, the lady. Evidently he's been calling her nonstop for the past couple of weeks—wouldn't get the hint. She finally changed her phone number, and he started showing up at her work."

Conner shook his head, not surprised. Domestic violence often escalated like this.

"She told him about the new boyfriend yesterday, thinking that would get him to move on. But evidently not," Seth continued. "She knew as soon as she saw him here this morning, he meant her physical harm."

Adrienne looked up at Seth from where she sat. "I'm glad you got here when you did, Seth. I really think he planned to shoot her. Shoot them both."

Seth grimaced. "Well, that's going to be hard to prove. But no matter what, she at least knows to be aware of her ex and keep away from him."

Conner walked over to help Adrienne out of her chair. He kept a hand at the small of her back in case she started to keel over again. "Are you ready to go?"

"Sure. Are we headed straight to the Bureau office?"

Conner looked down at Adrienne's clothes, splattered with coffee stains. "Do you want to go to your hotel first? Change clothes?"

"Yeah, that would be great." Adrienne smiled with relief.

"Do you want me to drive you or do you think you can walk? I'll walk with you. It's a couple of blocks, right?"

"Yeah, I should be fine to walk. Usually fresh air makes my head feel better."

"Usually?"

"Well, it just doesn't seem to hurt much at all now."

Conner noticed her confused look. "That's a good thing, right?"

"Yes, yes, I'm thankful," Adrienne responded quickly. "It has never…not hurt before. In a situation like this."

"Have you had many situations like this?" Seth asked her.

Adrienne looked away. "Enough. Not as many over the past few years."

Conner met Seth's eyes. They had a lot to talk about when Adrienne wasn't around. Not the least of which was what had happened here in this coffeehouse this morning. Adrienne obviously wasn't faking her physical reactions, and she had known that the perp meant harm to that woman.

It was looking more and more as though maybe she could do some of the stuff they'd heard she could do.

"All right, I'll take her to the hotel and let her change clothes, and then we'll meet you at the office, Seth." Conner looked at Adrienne's burnt arm. "Are you sure you're up for coming into the office today?"

Adrienne nodded. "I'll be fine."

"We'll stop at the drugstore on the way and get some gauze to protect the worst part of your burns."

Conner and Adrienne began walking toward the door. Seth told him that he would see them in a little while.

"Thank you," she said intently, grabbing his hand with her uninjured one.

"For what?"

"Believing me. For not asking for details and explanations I couldn't give at the time. For *acting* rather than allowing your natural doubts to cloud your instincts and demand more information."

Conner was stunned. That statement exactly summarized what had happened. The *instinct* had been to get her the assistance she needed immediately. He had almost let his doubt overshadow that gut reaction but didn't. And because of that, nobody had died today. Not the woman or her boyfriend or maybe even Adrienne.

Conner still wasn't sure what he believed Adrienne could or could not do in terms of "seeing" evil. But he was at least now willing to give her a chance.

Conner squeezed her hand. There were many things that probably could be said right now, but he wasn't sure which would be best or which might lead to an argument. So he said the only thing he could.

"You're welcome."

CONNER WAITED IN the lobby for Adrienne as she went up to her room and changed out of her coffee-soaked clothing. They had stopped at a corner drugstore to get Adrienne some ointment and gauze for the worst of her injuries.

The red blisters on her arm bothered Conner but on some level reassured him. Adrienne had obviously been in the grips of something…strange to be burned like that and not notice. And it was too extreme a measure for someone to act out in order to prove they weren't faking something. Adrienne had no reason to go that far, had nothing to gain by it.

Conner's phone buzzed in his pocket. It was Seth.

"Hey. You back at the office?" Conner asked, sitting on the armrest of one of the couches in the lobby.

"Yeah. Where are you guys?"

"We're at the hotel. Adrienne is up changing clothes. Finish everything okay on your end?"

"Yeah. Turned the ex over to the locals, and the lady is filing for a restraining order even as we speak."

Conner nodded. "Well, that's good." He and Seth both knew that a restraining order would not stop an ex-husband intent on doing the woman harm, but it was a start and at least made everything official.

"Her new boyfriend looked pretty spooked by the whole thing. Not sure how long that's going to last."

"Don't blame him." Conner chuckled ruefully.

"So it ends up that the coffeehouse had some closed-circuit video."

Conner stood up and walked outside, away from the few people in the lobby. "What did the CC feed show?"

"Mostly it was pointing at the counter and register, away from the action this morning. Didn't get the ex at all. But it caught Adrienne a couple times."

"And?"

Seth knew what Conner meant without explanation. "It was scary, man. Seriously. The people who described her as drunk? That's pretty accurate. And the coffee spill on her hand? That was spooky."

"I was just thinking about her burns, Seth. Burns

like that? Nobody does that to themselves on purpose to continue some stupid facade."

"You've got to see this footage. It was like something took over her body. She crushed that cup in her hand with a death grip. Didn't drop the cup or anything when it spilled on her. It was like she *couldn't* release it."

Conner rubbed his forehead and began pacing up the sidewalk. "What do you think, Seth? Does this mean she's legit? That she can really…whatever?"

"Con, all I know is that something happened to her in that restaurant this morning. You can literally see it overwhelm her. And it's not pretty. Damn scary."

Conner stopped his pacing. "But what does it mean?"

"I don't know. But she had no reason to fake it and no reason to know we would be watching. It leads me to believe she may be telling the truth, man."

Conner had never seen anything to make him think "gifts" like Adrienne's were possible.

He turned back toward the hotel and saw Adrienne walking out the lobby door. "Okay, I've got to go. Did you bring a copy of the CC footage back with you?"

Seth snorted. "Do you really have to ask? Of course. See you in a bit."

Conner hung up and walked toward Adrienne. She had changed into a khaki skirt and a white sleeveless blouse. Her short hair was a little damp from the shower she must have taken. Color had returned to her cheeks. She smiled, crossing to him.

She was breathtaking.

If only Conner knew that he could truly trust her.

Chapter Seven

Three hours later she was back in that same FBI inter-rogation room from yesterday. Adrienne sat, sure she was only minutes away from becoming a serial killer herself.

Nothing. She had absolutely nothing.

Staring at these pictures for the past hour and a half had brought not one single thought, feeling or insight. Just like yesterday. Like her gift had switched itself off. Again.

Although they didn't say anything, Adrienne knew Seth and Conner had to be at their wits' end with her. They had sat with her for the first hour as she went through the pictures. They had gotten her lunch but that didn't help. Then they had left; she assumed to do something more productive—which, let's face it, would be *anything* else.

She looked down at the crime scene pictures again. A dead woman, stabbed and left in a warehouse.

Nothing.

Adrienne stood from her chair in the interrogation room and leaned onto the table to stretch her back. The movement caused pain to shoot up her arm from the burns. It was a reminder that her gift had certainly worked well enough this morning. Why wasn't it working now?

A brisk knock on the door had Adrienne looking up from the table.

"Yes?"

In strolled Division Chief Logan Kelly. Adrienne recognized him right away. He had not changed much in the eight years since she had seen him last.

"Ms. Jeffries. It's good to see you again."

"Chief Kelly." Adrienne shook his outstretched hand but kept her greeting short.

That Adrienne didn't return the sentiment wasn't lost on the chief. He raised one eyebrow but said nothing.

"I understand you're having some difficulty using your profiling gift for this case."

"For some reason I can't seem to get insights on anything that has been shown to me so far."

The chief's eyebrow raised again. "Perhaps you just aren't trying hard enough." He sat down in the chair across the table from her.

Adrienne barely refrained from rolling her eyes and sat down herself. "I assure you, it is not for lack of effort."

"It seems like you never had this sort of problem when you worked for us before. It all came quite easily."

"Easily?" Adrienne gave a quiet cough of joyless laughter. "Although I may not have had this much difficulty in the past, there was never anything easy about what I did for the FBI."

Adrienne noticed rather smugly that her statement seemed to quiet Chief Kelly for the moment. She watched as he looked down at the pictures.

"Quite gruesome, aren't they?" he asked after a moment.

There was nothing Adrienne could do but agree. "Yes. Horrible."

"Don't you want to help stop whoever is doing this from killing more women, or do you just not care at all?"

Adrienne knew better than to be taken aback by the chief's abrupt tone but found herself feeling defensive anyway. "Chief Kelly, I'm not playing any games here. For whatever reason I'm just not able to get any insight into this case."

"Perhaps I should remind you that it is not you who has much at stake here, but your ranch manager, Rick Vincent."

Adrienne's eyes narrowed. "Yes, Chief. I am well aware of why I am here and what's at stake. And as much as I'd like to tell you to go to hell, I won't."

The chief sat back looking smug, but before he could respond, Adrienne continued in an angry tone. "And although you think you have some sort of hold over me now, Kelly, you don't. I may have been here yesterday because of what you think you can do to Rick Vincent if I don't cooperate. But I'm here right now because I want to help these women."

Adrienne stood and began sorting the pictures back into the correct files. Chief Kelly stood also and walked over to the interrogation room door.

Adrienne stopped him before he could leave. "But I want to make sure you understand this—I am not back to work for you. This is a one-shot deal, and I'm done. I'm older now, and I won't allow what happened to me before to happen again."

Chief Kelly surprised her by looking apologetic.

"Adrienne, we wouldn't let anything like that happen again. We could put measures in place to prevent it, to look out for your well-being."

"I thought that was true when I was eighteen years old—too young to know better. Now I know who I can trust. Myself," Adrienne all but scoffed.

Chief Kelly seemed about to respond when the door to the interrogation room burst open. Conner gave a momentary look at Adrienne, then turned to Chief Kelly.

"Chief, we just got a call. There's another victim."

Whatever Chief Kelly had been about to say to Adrienne was completely forgotten. "Simon?" the chief asked quietly.

Conner glanced at Adrienne, then turned back to the chief, nodding curtly.

"Did we receive another package?"

Conner glimpsed at her again and then away. Adrienne couldn't help but notice the way Conner posed himself with his back to her, which made it obvious that Adrienne was not a welcome part of this conversation.

"No, sir. Harrington and I are ready to proceed to the scene immediately."

"Okay, keep me posted." The chief excused himself quickly, and Conner turned to her.

"Seth and I have to leave for a little while."

"I understand."

"Do you want me to get someone to give you a ride back to the hotel?"

"No, I'll just stay, if that's okay."

Conner shifted uncomfortably. "That's fine. But I'll need you to stay in this room. If you have to leave, use the phone on the table to call the offices and someone will escort you."

"Don't want me wandering around on my own, huh?"

"Adrienne…" Conner took a step toward her.

Adrienne held her arm out to stop him. "No, it's fine. I'm not trustworthy. I get it. I haven't been of any use to you yet, anyway."

Conner sighed. "Adrienne, nobody's mad at you. It's okay if you can't…"

Adrienne cut him off. "I know you have to go. That's fine. I don't need to be placated. I'm just going to look over the pictures some more."

"Okay." Conner looked relieved as he walked to the door. "If it looks like we're going to be too long, I'll call and let you know so you're not just stuck here…"

Doing nothing.

Conner didn't say the words out loud, but Adrienne could hear them as sure as if he had spoken them.

He gave an apologetic shrug and walked out the door.

"Doing nothing" aptly described what Adrienne had accomplished here over the past day and a half. She glanced down at the pictures again. She didn't want to look at the brutal slayings anymore. Maybe she should just give it up, and head back to Vince and the horses.

Whatever Adrienne had been able to do for the FBI a decade ago, she was beginning to think she couldn't do it anymore.

She should be glad. Seeing Chief Kelly had reminded her of the pain she had gone through working for the FBI before. Just thinking of it now made her head begin to throb a little. Not being able to use her gift meant Adrienne wouldn't have to go through agony like the scene this morning at the coffee shop.

Adrienne sat and looked at the picture in her hands. It also meant she wouldn't be able to help catch the psycho who had horrifically murdered this beautiful young woman. Or stop him from killing anyone else.

Was it worth the pain—although calling it *pain* was really like calling a sumo wrestler chubby—if she knew she could help? That's what had kept her going for those two years, long past when any reasonable person could be expected to keep going. Knowing she could help.

Of course it looked like the decision was being made for her. She didn't seem to be able to help whether she wanted to or not.

And great, now *not* being able to help was starting to give her a headache.

Adrienne reached into her purse to grab a bottle of aspirin and then picked up one of the crime scene photos that had fallen to the floor. She glanced at it as she set it down on the table.

And all the images came screaming into her head.

The killer, with his knife, taunting the victims. Cutting locks of their hair to mail. His absolute glee at their terror. Knowing he had the power.

Adrienne put her hands up to her head, trying to hold it together and keep it from splitting into thousands of jagged pieces. As she looked at more pictures, thoughts from the killer became clearer.

He didn't kill them at the locations where they were found. He was much too smart for that. And the FBI agents were so stupid. It took them so long to catch on, he had to finally start sending them gifts. Bless their hearts.

Adrienne used all her concentration to block out the killer's feelings, instead trying to concentrate on useful information: a location, a time, thoughts about his appearance.

She could see a building with beams in the ceiling. Maybe a warehouse? A large cellar? There were no windows. This is where he brought them and where he kept them for a few hours before he killed them.

It was so hard to wait. He was in charge. He had the power. He tried to wait so the good feeling would last longer. Simon says, wait. But it was so hard.

It was like listening to a child whine. Adrienne tried to hold on to that. His thoughts were very childlike.

But holding on to anything with all the noise in her head was nearly impossible. The killer's malevolent thoughts were at the forefront, the loudest and most demanding. But pushing against her consciousness were other noises—other menacing forces, blurry ones with no distinct voices or sights—like someone was screaming at her in a different language. She knew she should be able to figure out what the noises meant, but it was too hard.

Adrienne persisted as long as she could, tried to gather as much information as possible in the screaming recesses of her mind. But eventually it overwhelmed her. She crawled over to the trash can—walking was impossible—and vomited the entire contents of the lunch she had eaten a little while before.

She dragged herself back to the table, pushing the pictures as far away from her as she could. She laid her head down on her arms on the table, closing her eyes. She just focused on breathing in and out, on trying to empty her mind of the noise and images.

This was what she remembered most about working with the FBI ten years before: the concentration it often took just to survive the next moment. Because trying to think about more than that was impossible.

Adrienne wasn't sure how long she lay with her head on the table. She thought it was hours, but she had been wrong before about that. She gingerly opened her eyes, delighted when the light didn't shoot agony into her head. She sat up slowly, expecting at any time for the images and sounds—and pain—to return, and was surprised when they didn't. Previously the only way to escape had been to physically remove herself from the area and any people.

Adrienne glanced at her phone. Conner had been gone for just over three hours. She wasn't sure when he was coming back, but she wanted to share what had happened as soon as she could. Some of it would help, surely.

She hoped so. She hated to think she had gone through that for nothing.

Although she had to admit she felt much better than she ever had before when she had worked for the FBI. Instead of the splitting headache and nausea she had expected, she just felt a little tired.

She wasn't brave enough to pick up the pictures that lay scattered all over the table and chair in case it instigated another physical onslaught. But she knew she had to remove the trash can where she had lost the contents of her stomach earlier. It wouldn't take much longer before the smell of that would overpower the tiny interrogation room.

Double-bagging and tying the small garbage sack, Adrienne headed out the door to look for a larger trash can. Despite the icky contents of the bag, the farther she got from the interrogation room, the better she felt. She saw a large trash can at the end of the hallway and headed to it.

She had just thrown away the bag when the elevator doors opened, and Conner and Seth exited, both looking annoyed and harried.

"What are you doing out here?" Conner snapped. "I thought I told you to stay in the interrogation room."

Adrienne was taken aback by his abrupt tone. "I needed to throw something away, so I stepped out for a few seconds."

Conner looked at her suspiciously. "Isn't there a trash can in the room?"

All the eagerness Adrienne had felt at sharing what she had discovered about Simon now disappeared with Conner's annoyance and disapproval. "Yes, there was, but the trash smelled bad so I took it out."

Adrienne didn't wait to hear Conner's response, just turned and headed back down the hallway.

He called after her anyway. "You're not supposed to leave the interrogation room without an escort!"

Adrienne ignored him. Jackass. After what she had been through this afternoon, she really didn't feel like putting up with him.

She made it all the way back to the interrogation room door before he caught up with her, grabbing her arm, but she noticed he was careful not to touch her burns.

"Did you hear me? I said you're not supposed to leave the interrogation room without somebody with you."

He had her at a distinct disadvantage—he towered a good ten inches over her five-foot-four frame. Adrienne had no doubt Conner Perigo knew exactly how to use his size to his advantage in intimidating others. But Adrienne wasn't going to let him bully her. She looked him dead in the eye.

"The. Trash. Smelled. Bad." She stood on tiptoe and accentuated each word with a poke to his chest. "So I took it out. It's the only time I've left the room for the entire time you've been gone."

Conner glowered down at her. "When you're in this building and I tell you to do something…"

"Ahem, excuse me, kids," Seth interrupted, sticking his head around Conner's shoulder. "Is everything okay here?"

Adrienne and Conner continued to scowl at each other.

"Any luck while we were gone, Adrienne?" Seth continued.

Adrienne smirked at Conner then turned to Seth. "Actually, Seth, yes. As soon as you guys left, my abilities started working. I think I may have a lot of information for you about Simon Says."

CONNER TOOK A step back when he heard the words *Simon Says* come out of Adrienne's mouth. Dammit, he *knew* they shouldn't have left her here alone, unsupervised. He didn't know how she'd done it, but somehow she had gotten pertinent information about the case. Information she shouldn't have known. Maybe she had chatted it out of some agents, or maybe she had gotten access to a file she shouldn't have been privy to.

Either way she now had information she shouldn't have.

Conner completely released Adrienne's arm. She immediately turned and went into the interrogation room. Seth began to follow her in. Conner didn't move.

"You coming?"

"In a minute. I need to get something from my desk. Don't start without me."

Conner could feel the anger building up inside him. He had to admit it was not all leveled at Adrienne. The crime scene they had just returned from had been an utter farce. When the call had come in that another woman's body had been found, he and Seth had hoped this was the break they were looking for. Finally a crime scene before they had gotten a package from Simon Says. But upon arrival at the location, it hadn't taken them long to figure out that this had not been Simon at all, but some sort of copycat. Too many differences, too much disorganization for it to be Simon.

Another waste of their time.

And then, as soon as they had returned, Conner finds Adrienne wandering all over the office, looking for a trash can? Seemed highly unlikely. And then she conveniently notifies them she has something to tell about the Simon Says case. A name she never could've known unless someone or something at this office had clued her in.

Conner walked over to his desk and grabbed a pen and ledger of paper. He and Seth would listen to what Adrienne had to say, but then they would send her back to her ranch. He didn't care what the chief said anymore. Conner was tired of being jerked around by dead ends.

Conner headed back to the interrogation room. He had wanted to believe Adrienne and her "abilities," especially after this morning. But he was tired of wasting time.

The smell hit him as he walked into the interrogation room. "Holy cow, what is that?"

Adrienne rolled her eyes at him. "I told you the trash smelled bad. That was why I was taking it out. You'll get used to it in a second."

Conner realized Seth was gone. "Where's Seth?"

"He went to get a can of air freshener."

"Thank God. What was in the trash?"

"I got sick to my stomach while you were gone."

Conner felt bad and let go of a little of his anger. "Oh, I'm sorry you got sick. Are you feeling better?"

"Yes. Surprisingly I feel pretty great."

Conner looked down at the photographs scattered all over the table. "Did you have a temper tantrum?" He gestured at them with his hand.

"No." Adrienne glared at him. "But I didn't want to touch them again, just in case."

"In case what?"

"In case I had the same reaction as I did the last time I looked at them."

Seth walked in and began spraying the room with freshener until it was difficult to breathe. But at least it smelled better.

Conner and Seth picked up the photos and sat across the table from Adrienne. He watched as Adrienne sat up straight in her chair and folded her hands lightly in her lap. She closed her eyes and took a deep breath.

Conner realized he was watching a ritual. She had done this before. Perhaps many times.

"Part of him thinks of this as a game," Adrienne began in a serious tone and then opened her eyes. "And he thinks you—the FBI—are stupid."

Conner and Seth looked at each other. They knew what Adrienne was saying was true. It was obvious from the mocking tone of the notes Simon had sent with the locks of hair.

Conner grimaced. If Adrienne knew this, it meant she had somehow accessed the files. That was more information than he wanted available to her.

"Go on," Seth encouraged.

"He's alternating between gleeful and whiny—like a young child. He likes to be in control, to terrify the women and prove he has power over them. He takes absolute delight in sending you the locks of hair."

Conner stayed still, but Seth sat back and whistled through his teeth. He obviously believed this was coming from Adrienne's "visions" rather than her accessing information while they were gone.

"No offense," Conner interrupted, "but you're not telling us anything that is not already in a file here. A file that perhaps got shown to you while we were gone."

That seemed better than accusing her of breaking into a desk.

"Agent Perigo."

Uh-oh, they were back to last names.

"Why would I do that? There's no point to it."

"I don't know, Ms. Jeffries. You tell me."

Conner felt Seth nudge him under the table. "Ignore him, Adrienne. Continue, please," Seth entreated.

"He keeps a separate lock of hair for himself. A trophy."

That was new. Of course, conveniently, there was no way to know if it was accurate.

"He places all the women at the locations where they are found, but he doesn't kill them there."

They knew this too—no blood had ever been found at any of the crime scenes.

"He kills them all at the same place—some sort of cellar or large empty room. It has a basement that's almost hidden. It's unusual. But there are no windows, and it has a ceiling with high dark rafters."

Conner now sat up straighter in his chair and saw Seth do the same out of the corner of his eye. This was something that they had never heard. It could potentially break open the case.

If they were willing to believe her.

"Can you remember anything else about the place?" Seth asked Adrienne.

She shook her head. "No, I'm sorry. I can only see this room. For some reason I can't see when he comes in or out of it, which would give us more to go on."

"Can you usually see stuff like that?" Conner asked.

Adrienne rubbed her forehead. "Usually. I'm sorry."

"What else can you tell us?"

Adrienne reached out to gather the five files of the dead women, where Conner and Seth had returned all the pictures. The files were blank on the front except for each woman's first name. Adrienne took the files and laid them out on the table.

"I know this was the order they were killed in," Adrienne told them without looking up from the files. Then she took a pen and proceeded to write the last name of the women on each of their files. "I know their names, also."

This was too much for Conner. Whatever she was doing, he was done playing her game. He stood up and grabbed the files from the table.

"You know what? I think that's just about enough." Conner was livid. "I don't know exactly what you're playing at here, but I don't have time for it. You obviously didn't stay in this room while we were gone today. I don't know which agent helped you or if you just broke into a desk. But I am done with this."

Adrienne stood with her hands leaning on the table, obviously upset. "Can I remind you, Agent Perigo, that *you* came to *me* and asked for my help? Oh, scratch that, I mean *blackmailed* me into helping. What possible reason could I have for making this stuff up?"

Conner mirrored Adrienne's stance on the table. "I have no idea, and I don't care anymore. Maybe you just want attention. Maybe you need to feel important. But the only way you could possibly know these things is if you got your hands on the case file or talked to someone else who did."

Adrienne slammed her small fist down on the table. "Unless—although I'm sure this is an unbearable thought for you to consider—I'm telling the truth!"

"Do you know that this room is equipped with video and audio recording equipment, Ms. Jeffries? It automatically starts digitally recording whenever someone is in here."

"So?" She continued to glare at him from across the table.

"So? It will certainly show any time you left this room or anyone who came to see you while we were gone. And anything that was said."

Conner wasn't sure exactly what he expected Adrienne to do with this information. Change her story maybe. Start crying. Try to make up some excuse for the information she had.

He definitely didn't expect how she actually responded.

"Well, I guess I know how you'll be spending your next three hours, Special Agent Jackass. But I'm leaving."

She reached down to get her purse—he saw her wince when her burned arm scraped the chair—then stormed out of the room, slamming the door.

Conner stared at the closed door for a long time. Beside him, he heard Seth begin to chuckle. Conner muttered something unrepeatable under his breath and headed out the door to look at the recorded footage of Adrienne. But he suddenly didn't feel as sure as he had just a few minutes before.

Chapter Eight

The great thing about San Francisco was all the parks, Adrienne thought as she walked around in one of them. You couldn't walk half a block without running into some little grassy area or square. And the weather hovered around sixty degrees all year long in San Fran. Gorgeous.

The bad thing about San Francisco? All the jerky FBI agents who made her want to tear her hair out. Either that or jump across the table and kiss him until neither of them could breathe.

Adrienne smiled. At least if she kissed Conner, she wouldn't have to listen to any of the asinine statements that seemed to pour endlessly from his mouth.

Adrienne sat down on a bench. The buzzing was back. She wasn't sure exactly when it had started up again, but it was there. And a headache was coming on—pressure surrounding the back of her skull. Annoying but bearable.

This was the headache she was used to having when she was around people. The constant distant buzzing. Nothing bad; nothing to see or hear. Just light static. She had found over the years that most people were not evil. They may be tired or cranky or just plain mean.

But most did not walk around with sinister intentions, so Adrienne never had any clear idea of their thoughts. Just low static.

Usually being outside helped a bit—fewer people than were cooped up in buildings—but now it seemed worse than when she had been in the FBI field office.

Maybe being annoyed at Conner Perigo had helped her forget about her headache. But when she thought about it, she realized, no, she hadn't really had any sort of headache—or any pain at all—since she had taken the trash out of the interrogation room. That was so unusual.

But the pain was making its way back now, that was for sure. Adrienne reached into her purse and got out aspirin from the bottle she always kept with her. This would help keep the headache in check, to a degree.

Adrienne sat in the sun for a little while then decided to take a walk down to the Embarcadero—San Francisco's waterfront area. It had a beautiful view—the Golden Gate Bridge and Alcatraz—but Adrienne barely noticed it.

Why was she so angry at Conner Perigo? It wasn't as if she hadn't had to prove herself before. Nobody believed what she could do at first. She had always accepted that as reasonable. What sane person would believe her without proof?

And her gift had been so sketchy over the past couple of days. Why should she expect Conner to just believe what she could do out of hand? And more than that, Adrienne had *never* cared who had believed her in the past. Why was she starting to now?

There was something about Conner Perigo that was different. Adrienne didn't know really what it was, but she knew she hadn't been able to stop thinking about him from the first moment she had seen him in the barn two days ago. And the kiss at the hotel last night. She had thought they had turned some sort of corner then.

But evidently Agent Perigo didn't actually have to trust or believe her in order to act on his attraction to her. The kiss obviously hadn't implied he had feelings for her, because feelings were based on trust, and Perigo most definitely didn't trust her.

Of course Adrienne could also admit to herself that whatever she felt for Conner didn't come wrapped up in a nice little bow, either. She seemed to spend most of the time she was around him fighting the urge to slap the smug look off his face. But she definitely had to admit that he affected her. She wasn't sure what she was going to do about that.

Adrienne knew he would watch the footage from the interrogation room and know she was telling the truth. Where things would go from there—professionally and personally—she had no idea. She wasn't sure what she wanted.

It wasn't long before Adrienne realized coming down to the Embarcadero hadn't been a good idea. It was much more crowded. The buzzing was becoming louder and her headache worse. Adrienne bought a pretzel from a vendor—to replace the lunch she had lost before, and hopefully to ward off some nausea now—and decided to begin walking back toward the FBI building.

She stopped at another park and nibbled on her pretzel for a few moments before giving up. Her headache was definitely worse, and she doubted she'd be able to keep any food down long. Adrienne put her hand up to her forehead to try to shade her eyes and give her head some relief from the pain the sunlight was causing, even though it wasn't a particularly bright day out.

This was what she remembered from her years with the FBI. The constant bombardment. Even when she was out of the office with no one asking her to look at some crime scene photo or touch some artifact, she still had never been able to get any quiet in her head. When she was eighteen and nineteen, she had thought she could just push through the pain and the noise and keep going.

She had been wrong.

It hadn't seemed so bad earlier today, but now Adrienne just felt like hell. She would go back to the office, tell Conner and Seth that she was heading to the hotel. Maybe she'd even drive back to Lodi tonight. At least there she knew she'd have some peace. But she definitely needed to get away and give her body a chance to rest and heal. She couldn't keep this up for long.

That she knew from experience.

Plus, if her gifts were only going to work every once in a while, then she really wasn't going to be much help to the FBI at all. So she might as well go.

From where she sat on the park bench, she heard the car pull up to the curb—tires slightly squealing—and saw it at the same time. She watched as Conner Perigo got out of the car and strode with determination straight toward her bench.

Adrienne looked down at her watch. She'd been gone about forty-five minutes. That was quicker than she had thought. She'd figured it would take him longer to go through the footage.

"How did you find me?" Adrienne picked at her pretzel some more as he sat down beside her without saying anything.

Conner cleared his throat in an embarrassed fashion. "I had them track your phone's GPS."

"Special Agent Perigo, I'm shocked. Isn't that a mis-use of taxpayers' money?"

"Probably. I thought you were already gone, maybe headed back to Lodi. If I had known you were only a few blocks away, I wouldn't have driven."

"So you found me." Adrienne put another small piece of pretzel in her mouth. "I would've thought it would take longer to go through all that footage of me in the interrogation room. They must have a fast for-ward switch, huh?"

Conner shifted uncomfortably on the bench. "Look, Adrienne…"

Adrienne took that as a yes. He trailed off, obviously waiting for Adrienne to say something, but she wasn't about to make this easy for him. "Yes?"

"I'm sorry, okay? I was wrong."

"You saw the footage?"

"Yes, some of it."

Adrienne cocked an eyebrow at him. Only some?

"Okay, most of it. Enough to know you were obvi-ously telling the truth. You didn't leave and nobody came in."

"Where's Seth?"

Conner looked away sheepishly. "He stayed to watch the rest of the footage, just in case."

Adrienne shook her head. "You have real trust is-sues, you know that?"

"Occupational hazard, I guess."

They sat in silence for a moment before Conner spoke again. "I lost my temper, and I was wrong. When we left today, we rushed to that crime scene thinking it was a big break in the case only to find out it wasn't Simon at all. A copycat. When I got back I was in a bad mood already. Then when I saw you in the hall-way, I just lost it."

Adrienne peeked over at him, turning toward him slightly. She wasn't ready to let him off the hook yet, but she could at least understand how the copycat killer would've put him on edge.

Conner slid a little closer to Adrienne. When she didn't move away, he put his arm along the back of the bench, touching her shoulders.

"That still doesn't excuse how I behaved. What I said. I *am* a jackass. I'm sorry."

"You know, it's okay to be incredulous. Usually I'm not offended by skepticism." Adrienne broke off another piece of her pretzel and began to eat it, realizing she was now starving.

"I want you to know, it's not you personally I'm critical of." Conner hesitated as he seemed to try to find the right words. "It's just that I have no script for what you can do. No way to categorize it and hardly know how to process it."

Adrienne nodded as she chewed. Not being able to categorize her gift was something she understood.

"This is hard for me," Conner continued. "But after what happened to you this morning and this afternoon, I can't doubt you anymore. But I don't know how to explain what you can do or how you can do it."

"Sometimes there doesn't have to be an explanation. It just is what it is," Adrienne said softly.

Conner turned toward Adrienne on the bench. "Your abilities fly in the face of normal reason. It goes against everything I've learned in all my years of law enforcement," he said in a tone gentler than she would've thought him capable of when discussing this topic.

"I'm sure that's not as true as you think," Adrienne

assured him. "Haven't you ever followed a hunch and found it to be valid? My abilities aren't so different than that. Just more well developed."

"Yeah, but yours are a little more hocus-pocus."

Adrienne smiled, unoffended. "It's not like my mother slept with Thor or that gypsies cursed my family or something. I just have a talent."

Conner snorted. "I heard what you said today. Things you saw and know? It's quite a bit more than a talent."

"My brain just works differently than most people. Like how some kids taught themselves how to play the violin when they were five years old and had never heard the instrument before. I'm kind of a prodigy, but I'm not a freak."

Freak was a sensitive word for her. It was why she had always hated the nickname Bloodhound. Too close to freak.

Conner reached over and ran the backs of his fingers down her cheek. "Not a freak. Never. Your brain is different and can do special things."

"I'm a terrible speller," Adrienne said softly.

"You can't spell?"

Conner was still stroking her cheek. Adrienne smiled. "No, not at all. I have to think about the difference between *there, they're* and *their* for five minutes before I figure out which is correct."

"Okay, maybe a little bit of a freak." Conner smiled and closed the distance between them, cupping the back of her head with his hand.

His lips were firm but gentle, and Adrienne was immediately swept up in the kiss. She felt Conner's other hand come up to frame her face as she leaned closer to him, her hands tracing his arms from his elbows up to his shoulders.

Adrienne gave herself over to the kiss, drowning in it. It was like yesterday's kiss—overwhelming. All she could feel was Conner. There was no buzzing, no static in her head, only Conner.

Adrienne's eyes flew open.

No buzzing. No headache. Silence.

Nothing.

Adrienne jumped off the bench, out of Conner's arms, ignoring his shocked gaze. She shook her head as if to clear it and concentrated hard, trying to pick up on the buzz that she should hear from the other people in the park—the static. She looked around; there were at least a dozen people. She should hear them.

Her eyes spun back to Conner.

She watched wariness enter his gorgeous green eyes. "You're not going to start calling me Agent Jackass again, are you? That's starting to get around the office."

"What did you do to me?"

"I…kissed you?"

Adrienne could tell Conner wasn't sure how to handle her strange reaction. She didn't blame him. She knew she was acting abnormally, but something was wrong here.

"You've done something to me." Adrienne shook her head again, as if to unclog something.

"Well, my kisses have been known to cause a commotion in many a lady," Conner joked.

"It's you. You're the problem." Adrienne threw herself back down on the bench looking at him with wide eyes.

"What?" Conner obviously had no idea what she was talking about.

"Wait. I have to think." Fortunately thinking was much easier without the noise and headache.

When she had worked with the FBI before, the pain from her gift had been a constant. Only when she could physically remove herself from people had she had any relief from the noise and discomfort. But since she had come back to help Conner and Seth, she'd experienced some pain, but not constantly. And her abilities had worked, but not constantly.

Adrienne looked down at the burn on her arm. Her gift had worked this morning at the coffeehouse—she remembered the excruciating pain in her head. She had even gotten a nose bleed. Then she had passed out and felt better when she woke up. No headache at all, just the pain from the burn.

Conner had been there with her when she had woken up.

And at the field office today, nothing seemed to work when she was looking at the pictures of the murders, until Conner and Seth had been called away. Once they were gone, it had completely overwhelmed her. Images, sounds, the thoughts of the killer. And the agony that came with them.

All gone away again once Conner was back.

Adrienne remembered when she had first laid eyes on Conner two days ago. She had walked into the barn and was absolutely shocked to see someone standing in there besides Vince. Vince's buzz was a constant that she was so used to she totally didn't notice it anymore. But other people's should've been evident. Adrienne remembered how taken aback she had been at the silence, although it hadn't been long before Conner had made her so angry she hadn't even noticed the quiet.

Conner. It kept coming back to Conner.

He was looking at her expectantly, although she had to give him credit, he had waited quietly like she had asked him to. Adrienne reached over and grabbed his hand in hers.

"Do I need to apologize for kissing you?" he asked warily.

Adrienne smiled shyly. "No."

"Good, because I don't think I can. You want to fill me in with what's going on?"

"I think I know what's wrong with me."

"What are you talking about? I already told you, there's nothing wrong with you."

Adrienne shook her head. "I mean, what's wrong with my abilities. Why they didn't work yesterday but are working today. Sometimes."

"I don't understand. What did you figure out?"

"It's just a theory." Adrienne hesitated. She could be wrong, and she didn't want to make him mad. She should find out for sure first, before she said anything to him.

Adrienne looked down at her hand that rested on his. Hers looked so small and frail compared to his big capable hands.

"It's okay, just tell me."

Adrienne gripped his hand harder. "I need you to do something for me."

"Sure. What?"

Adrienne reached up and put her hands on either side of his cheeks. She leaned over and kissed him. She meant it to be just a quick peck, but her plans to distract him evaporated as soon as her lips touched his. She felt his arms come around her and draw her closer. She sighed and gave herself over to the kiss.

Her lips opened when she felt his tongue, and she slanted her head to give him more access. Her fingers slid up into his hair as she pulled him closer. It was Conner who broke away after a few moments.

"Um, Adrienne, we're in a park, baby. And I'll probably lose my job if I get arrested for public indecency."

Adrienne giggled softly. "Sorry."

Conner brushed his lips with hers again softly. "A giggle. Quite the beautiful sound."

"I'm not much of a giggler."

Conner's lips brushed hers again. "Maybe you should consider becoming one."

"Maybe."

"So, Ms. Jeffries, what's your theory? What do you need me to do?"

Adrienne took a deep breath and put her forehead against Conner's.

"I need you to get away from me. As soon as possible."

Conner pulled back from her immediately. "What?"

"I just need you to go away from me for a little bit while I check a couple things out," Adrienne responded as gently as she could.

"Why can't I come with you? Where am I supposed to go?"

"This is something I have to do alone to test my theory. And you can go wherever you want. Go to your house or my hotel or Golden Gate Park. Wherever. I just need you to not be near me for a while."

Adrienne could tell Conner didn't understand and was struggling with her request. She knew he wanted to demand more answers and appreciated his restraint.

"Please, Conner. Just for a little while. Call Seth and have him meet me in the lobby of the field office. It won't take me long to figure it out."

Conner shook his head and stood up. "Okay, fine. But I don't like this."

Adrienne stood up onto her tiptoes and kissed him on the cheek. "I know." She smiled at him. "But thank you for doing it anyway."

Conner ran his fingers down Adrienne's cheek. "I'll do it as long as you promise to explain to me what's going on as soon as you can."

Adrienne nodded. "I promise."

Conner turned and began walking to his car. "I'm going to head to my house since I left there before six this morning. A shower would probably do me good."

"Thank you, Conner," Adrienne called out to him.

"Call me soon." Conner opened the driver's-side door but didn't get in. Instead, he looked at her over the roof of his car. Adrienne was entranced by his intent stare. "And, Ms. Jeffries? No matter what your theory is, we're going to finish what got started here this afternoon. And when we do, it won't be in a park."

Adrienne couldn't think of anything to say to that. Lord, she hoped they did get a chance.

"Seth will be waiting for you in the lobby," Conner called out to her as he got in his car and pulled away.

Adrienne quickly began walking back to the FBI field office. The sooner she got this done, the sooner she could take Agent Perigo up on his offer.

Chapter Nine

Adrienne found Seth waiting for her when she walked into the FBI office a few minutes later. She could already feel tension building up in her head, but told herself that it didn't prove anything definitively.

"Hey." Seth smiled at her. "Glad you didn't leave for good."

"No. I was just trying to get some air."

"Conner called but didn't give me very much detail about what we're doing right now."

"I know. That's because I didn't give him much detail. Let's just say I'm testing a theory." She cocked her head toward the elevators, and they began walking.

"Theory about what?"

"My abilities."

Seth hit the button for the elevator. "Okay. Anything particular about them?"

"Why they seem to be a little hit-or-miss lately. They've never been that way before."

The elevator door opened, and they walked inside. Seth pushed the number for the floor their offices were on. "So, what's the plan?"

Adrienne turned and looked straight at Seth. "I'm

going to ask you to do something you might not want to do. But it's kind of important."

"What's that?"

The elevator chimed, and the doors opened. Adrienne stepped out and began walking down the hallway. She could already hear the buzzing, and her headache was definitely back. "I need you to show me one of Simon's packages."

"Okay."

Adrienne was a bit taken aback. She had expected more resistance from Seth. "Just like that?"

"Yep."

"Do you think Conner will be mad when he finds out?" Adrienne wondered aloud.

"Nope. He's the one who told me to give you access to whatever you need."

Adrienne stopped midstride. "Really?"

Seth half smiled at her. "Yep. Do you think he's been abducted by aliens?"

"Probably." Adrienne snickered. But she was so pleased. This was a huge step for Conner, she knew. She began walking again.

"Where do you want to go? Back to the interrogation room again?" Seth asked.

The buzzing was getting worse and taking on more definite form, like there were whispers coming from within the walls all vying for her attention. This building was, of course, a place where evil was investigated every day. Definitely no lack of menacing and threatening people here. The images and sounds seemed to want to jump from the rooms and throw themselves into Adrienne's mind.

Adrienne rubbed her forehead and concentrated just

on walking. "Yeah, let's go back there. At least I'm familiar with that room."

Seth told her that he would meet her there in minute, and Adrienne went inside. The room had been cleaned out since she had left earlier that afternoon. She sat down at the now-empty table. She could still hear all the whispers, see vague visions of violence as she waited for Seth to return.

Adrienne breathed in through her nose and out through her mouth to try to keep herself focused, a practice she had learned in a yoga class. It didn't really help, but at least it gave her something to do.

Seth walked in holding a box. He set it on the table in front of her. It was a small brown box, about half the size of a shoe box. Plain. Unassuming. It looked so benign, like millions of packages that get mailed daily all over the world.

Adrienne was terrified to touch it, but she knew there was no point in waiting.

Touching as little of the box as she could, she pulled back the flaps on the top. Inside was a small jeweler's box that a necklace might come in. Adrienne flinched as she reached in and pulled the smaller box out of the package.

She could feel her breath sawing in and out of her lungs. She forced herself to open the jeweler's box. Inside it was a lock of hair. She reached down and touched it gently.

Every muscle in her body tightened unbearably. The force of what she was feeling threw her back into the chair. She still had some of the lock of hair caught between her fingers.

Adrienne began sobbing as all of the killer's thoughts overwhelmed her mind. She could tell Seth was trying to say something to her, felt him touching her arm and shaking her, but he seemed so far away—outside the impenetrable wall of the killer's ominous thoughts.

All the killer's feelings piled on top of each other in a hideous cacophony within Adrienne's head. She focused her energy on trying to sort through them, to pick out useful information, but the effort was too great. It was like the killer was in the room with them, his presence was so strong.

Adrienne forced her fingers to release the lock of hair, but that gave her only the slightest reprieve. She brought her hands up to her head, pressing her palms hard into her eyes.

Adrienne knew she should touch the hair again; should keep going. After all, this was what she had been hoping for, right? For her abilities to work? But this was different—the intensity was so much greater than before.

Adrienne touched the hair again, trying to brace herself against the mental anguish, but it didn't help. The noise in her head sky-rocketed. She fell against the table and could feel blood begin to drip from her nose. She let go of the hair, but it didn't seem to help at all.

Adrienne couldn't take this anymore; she had to get away—just for a while. She would mentally refortify then come back. But for right now she had to get away. She looked over for Seth but found he was gone. In the back of her mind, Adrienne knew there was something she was trying to do but remembering was too much effort.

She had to get out of this building. Where was Seth? She couldn't take time to look for him. The elevator was just a few yards down the hall. Surely she could make it there and then outside. Away from this package and this killer.

Away from this evil.

Adrienne hoisted herself out of the chair and walked unsteadily to the door. It took her a few moments to remember how to turn a doorknob. She pulled the door with as much strength as she could muster, but the opening was so small she could barely slide through.

The hallway was a twisted carnival fun house, seeming to stretch on endlessly. Leaning heavily on the wall, Adrienne concentrated on putting one foot in front of the other. She could hear sounds, words, but she didn't know if it was actual people talking to her or the evil in her head, so she ignored them.

Just making it to the elevator used all Adrienne's strength. She pressed the button on the wall and sobbed with relief when the elevator doors opened immediately. She heard shouting and saw Seth's concerned face just as the doors closed.

Strength gone, Adrienne leaned her back against the elevator wall and slid to the ground heavily. She reached up and pressed the lowest button without looking, hoping it would take her to the ground floor. From there she would crawl out if necessary.

As soon as the elevator started moving, Adrienne felt better. She was going to make it. The noise and pain were already lessening. The dimness that had threatened her vision was receding.

The elevator dinged, and the door opened. There stood Conner, tension outlining every muscle in his body. He dropped down next to her immediately.

"Conner…" Adrienne reached for him.

For the second time that day, Adrienne fell unconscious into his arms.

THIS WAS BECOMING a pattern. Conner caught Adrienne before she fell to the ground. Seth's panicked call to him a few minutes ago had Conner racing back into town, breaking all sorts of traffic laws—just like this morning—to get back to Adrienne.

By the looks of Adrienne, Seth hadn't been exaggerating. She looked like absolute hell. She had no color whatsoever and seemed to be shivering uncontrollably even though it wasn't cold in the building.

The elevator started protesting at having the door opened too long, so Conner let it close. He brushed back a couple errant strands of short hair that had fallen over her forehead. Adrienne murmured and started to move.

"Hey, sweetheart," Conner whispered. "You ready to wake up?"

Just a few moments later her big hazel eyes opened.

"It's you." She hesitated for a few moments then smiled at him.

"Yep, it's me."

"No, I mean it is you who affects me this way. The pain is gone. And the noise."

Adrienne began to get up from her place on the elevator floor. Conner reached down to help her. "Are you sure you're okay to get up? It's fine to rest longer if you need to."

She smiled at him again. "No, I feel fine. So much better than I did a few minutes ago. Seth is probably worried about me. We should go see him."

Conner pressed the button on the elevator, and they began to go up again. When the doors opened, Seth was there, concern radiating from him.

"Oh, thank God. Are you all right, Adrienne? You looked like absolute, god-awful death when you stumbled into that elevator."

Adrienne rolled her eyes. "Thanks."

"I'm serious. I think I aged ten years watching what just happened to you. Are you okay? You do look much better now, I have to admit. What happened?"

Adrienne stuck her thumb out toward Conner. "He happened."

Conner looked down at her, confused. "That's the second time you've alluded to me. What are you talking about?"

Conner led her down the hall, away from the interrogation room. Instead they went into the main section of offices. He sat Adrienne in his desk chair and perched on the corner of his desk. Seth pulled up another chair near them.

"I noticed it earlier this afternoon," Adrienne explained, huddling back in the chair.

"What exactly?" Conner asked.

"Whenever I'm around you, my abilities don't work."

Conner was taken aback. "What? Why? Why would you think that?"

Adrienne shrugged. "I don't know why. Think about it—every time you've been around me I haven't been able to do anything to help with the case."

Conner glanced over at Seth. He shrugged.

"And whenever you aren't around me, everything does work—like at the coffeehouse this morning."

Conner wasn't convinced. "That still doesn't mean…"

"And this afternoon, it was only after you guys had gone to the crime scene and were away from this building that I got anything from looking at the pictures."

Conner wasn't sure how to feel about this information. Adrienne reached over and touched his hand. "I can't hear or sense anything when you're around. Like right now, there's silence—no buzzing, no static, no voices or images pushing at me. No pain. And in this building, with all the case files and evidence, that's pretty unbelievable."

"But bad." Conner frowned.

She squeezed his hand. "Not for me." She smiled softly at him.

He squeezed her hand in return. "But what does this mean?"

"I don't know." She let go of his hand and sat back in the chair. "But I'm grateful I'm not vomiting and throwing back pain relievers like candy."

Conner still wasn't sure what all this meant or the ramifications if what Adrienne suggested was true. He decided to focus on what he did know. "Tell me what happened while I was gone earlier. Were you able to pick up anything?"

Adrienne nodded.

"I showed her the package from Josie Paton."

Josie Paton, the most recent victim, found in an abandoned building two weeks ago. Married, age thirty-one.

Conner looked at Adrienne. "Did you get anything when you saw the package?"

She flinched and drew in her breath. "He was mad at her because she refused to be scared. She couldn't fight, because he had her restrained, but she would curse at him and call him names."

Adrienne stopped, but Conner knew there was more. "You can tell us, Adrienne. Just go ahead and say it."

Conner listened for a long time as Adrienne told them details of the murder and the abduction. Things she would have no possible way of knowing without her abilities to understand the killer's mind and his reasoning.

"I still can't get a good picture of where he's taking them when he first grabs them. I don't know why that is."

"Why is he choosing these particular women?" Conner asked. Their physical size seemed to be the only similarity. He and Seth had checked and double checked to see if there were any other ties between the women: where they shopped, ate, worked, exercised. They couldn't find anything.

Adrienne rubbed her forehead wearily. "They remind him of someone—a woman he knew. But I'm not sure who that person is to him. It seems to float in and out of his mind, and I can't get a hold on it."

Adrienne shifted uncomfortably in her chair, and Conner really looked at her. She seemed exhausted, on the verge of utter collapse. Conner wasn't surprised; it had been a long, physically difficult day for her. She needed a break.

"Hey, why don't we give it rest for a little while? There's a couch in the conference room where you can lie down. I just need to go over a few things with Seth, then I'll take you back to the hotel."

Adrienne smiled up at him gratefully. Conner offered both hands out to her which she took to help herself out of the chair. He grabbed his jacket from the back of it and led Adrienne to the conference room. She immediately sank heavily onto the couch.

Conner squatted down and draped his jacked over her. She smiled, snuggling into it.

"I'm just going to rest for a few minutes," she said as her eyes began to close.

Conner couldn't stop himself from reaching over to stroke her cheek. "That's fine, sweetheart. No one will disturb you here."

By the depth of her breathing, he doubted she even heard him.

Two hours later Conner and Seth had thoroughly revetted the Josie Paton file, adding and cross-referencing all the information Adrienne had provided. Although it didn't give them any immediate leads, it did provide a better overall understanding of who—and what—they were dealing with.

For the first time in ten months Conner felt a sense of hope. They were going to catch this psycho. Adrienne's help was going to be key.

After going through the file, Seth showed Conner the video footage of Adrienne opening Simon's package. Conner watched in barely concealed horror at the physical reaction the package had on Adrienne. There was no way something like that could be faked. He looked on as her muscles seemed to lock up. All color left her face. Touching the lock of hair in Simon's package seemed to almost hurl her across the room.

Conner watched as Adrienne tried to control it, closing her eyes and breathing.

He looked over at Seth who studied the screen, blankly shaking his head. "She scared the hell out of me, man. I am not kidding. I couldn't get her to come out of it. That's when I called you."

Conner turned back to the screen as Adrienne fought with what she was seeing and feeling for a long time to determine who would get control. It was almost as if she were in a trance. Then her eyes jerked open, and she started walking for the door.

If walking is what you could call it. It was more like dragging her own body.

"That's when she headed for the elevator," Seth whispered.

They both watched in horror as it took her minutes to figure out what a three-year-old child could do in two seconds: turn the handle of the door. She opened it as far as she seemed able, then squeezed through. And out of the sight of the camera.

Seth and Conner both sat back in their chairs, exhausted from just having viewed that. Neither spoke. What could be said?

Conner knew he had to get her out of this building. Whether he blocked—he mentally scoffed at that term—her abilities or not, he did not want her here one more minute.

He turned to Seth. "I'm taking her back to the hotel. I can't stand the thought of her here anymore."

"I totally agree. I'll see you tomorrow."

Conner went back into the conference room where Adrienne still slept. She had curled both legs under his jacket and had one arm tucked under her cheek on the armrest. Dark circles still framed her eyes. Conner hated to wake her up but knew she would be more comfortable sleeping back at the hotel.

"Hey, Sleeping Beauty, ready to wake up?" He touched her shoulder gently.

Her eyes fluttered open, then she sat straight up on the couch. Conner could tell she was trying to get her bearings. She brought her hands to her head, almost as a reflex, then slowly lowered them.

"How long have I been asleep?" she finally asked.

"A couple hours. Not long. I'm done here for the day and thought I would take you to the hotel."

Adrienne stood and stretched. "Okay, that sounds good. I don't usually fall asleep in busy places—too much buzzing. But I'm still tired anyway."

They returned to the interrogation room to grab Adrienne's purse and were soon in the parking garage, getting into Conner's car.

"I've been thinking about me blocking your abilities," Conner started as they pulled out of the garage.

"I'd be more comfortable if you'd call them my freakishly awesome crime-fighting superpowers. But please continue."

Conner chuckled. If Adrienne was back to wisecracking, then she was feeling much better. "Why do you think *I* block your superpowers? Does that happen often?"

It took Adrienne so long to answer, Conner wasn't sure she was going to. "Honestly, I don't know why you block them. The only other time this has happened is with my sisters..." She faded off.

"You have sisters?"

"Yes. One older, one younger. But I don't see them very often."

"Why not?"

"Our parents died when I was twelve. There wasn't any other family to take us in, and we ended up in the foster system. Trying to find a family to take three traumatized preteen girls with special needs became impossible. So we wound up in different homes." Adrienne shrugged.

Conner grimaced. First she'd lost her parents, then her sisters. Not easy. But he caught an interesting turn of phrase.

"Special needs? As in 'freakishly awesome crime-fighting superpowers' special needs?"

"Sort of."

"Do they have abilities like you do?"

"Yeah, but not exactly the same."

Conner waited for Adrienne to say more, but it became apparent that discussing her sisters' special needs/ freakishly awesome abilities was not on the table. "But they block your ability, too?"

"Yes, when the three of us are together, we block each other out. But we don't really know why."

Adrienne obviously didn't want to talk about her sisters, so Conner changed the subject. "Was using your superpowers always this painful when you worked for the FBI before? Seth showed me the footage from this afternoon when you opened the package."

"Well, I have to admit, I'm out of practice. I was mentally tougher back then, better able to focus and protect myself. But I'm not sure that anything could've prepared me for that package today. The evil was so *immediate*. So close." Adrienne shuddered. "But, yeah, it always hurt."

Conner shook his head. "Why didn't you tell someone about the physical pain? You were a teenager, for heaven's sake. Somebody could've helped you. Done something."

"Conner, I did tell people. Including Chief Kelly. It's not like I could hide it. Half the time I was vomiting my guts out or walking around with a bloody nose."

Conner ground his teeth. How could Chief Kelly— hell, how could anybody at the Bureau—allow a teenager to be abused in such a way?

"The FBI weren't monsters. I realize that now," Adrienne responded as if Conner had spoken the thought aloud. "There just was always a critical case. Always *one more case* that needed the abilities of the Bloodhound, before I took a break."

Conner grimaced. He didn't like it, but he at least understood. How much pain would he be willing to allow someone to go through if it meant saving the lives of the women Simon Says was killing?

Even worse, what if you were the one who had to choose how much agony you would endure in order to help people in dire situations? How did an eighteen-year-old make a decision like that?

"So you quit?" Conner asked. He didn't blame her.

"No, I finally had a complete breakdown and ended up in the hospital for six weeks. Then I quit."

Yep, that would do it. Conner drove in silence as Adrienne stared out the window.

"I just couldn't take it anymore after that," Adrienne whispered. "I was afraid working for the Bureau would end up killing me."

Conner could hear the regret in her voice; she obviously considered herself a coward for the choice she had made. He reached over and linked his fingers with hers.

"Hey, no one could blame you for making the choice you did. It doesn't do any good to have you help others if you barely live through it yourself."

She looked down at their linked hands then smiled sadly at him. "Maybe." Her voice was still small.

Conner pulled into a parking spot at her hotel. He turned off the engine but didn't get out of the car. He released his seat belt and turned toward her.

"Adrienne, you were so young. Someone—Chief Kelly, or, hell, any of the agents—should've seen what was happening to you and done something about it."

Adrienne shrugged and looked away. Conner let go

of her hand and put his hands on either side of her cheeks, drawing her gaze back to him.

"After what I saw with you today, I would not blame you if you never set foot in a Bureau office again. Nobody would. You're not a coward, Adrienne. The fact that you're still here helping us proves that."

She was stronger than she knew and more beautiful than he could stand. He bent his head down to hers and kissed her. The kiss was soft and almost sweet at first, but as Conner felt her respond, he deepened the kiss. Her hands slid up to his chest, and he pulled her closer.

They had kissed before, but this time Conner was aware of how fragile Adrienne really was. How tiny she was in his arms. When the tip of Conner's tongue outlined Adrienne's lips, she sighed very softly. The sound sent a shiver through him. Conner felt Adrienne's fingers curling into his shirt and cursed the restricting confines of the car. Conner didn't want to leave Adrienne's lips even for the little time it would take to walk inside and up to her room.

The sudden ringing of Adrienne's phone was jarring in the relative silence of the car. Breathing heavy, Conner pulled away from her lips slowly. Adrienne had a slightly dazed look.

"I think that's your phone," Conner finally said after the third ring.

Adrienne fished the phone out of the bag. "It's Vince at the ranch. I have to take this. I'm sorry." She answered the phone and told Vince to hold on for a moment.

Conner ran his fingers down Adrienne's cheek. "It's been a long day for us both. I'll just see you tomorrow. I'll come by and pick you up for breakfast."

Adrienne turned her head to the side and kissed his

palm then smiled and got out of the car. Conner watched until she was safely inside the hotel, then started the ignition and pulled away. It really had been a long day for both of them.

And Conner had a feeling the long days were just getting started.

Chapter Ten

The next morning Conner picked Adrienne up at the hotel, they had breakfast and went into work. As soon as they got in the Bureau office, Conner could tell something had happened. It didn't take them long to find out what.

Another package had arrived from Simon Says.

It had already been vetted by security and held no threats to the FBI team in terms of its physical contents. All that was left to do now was open it.

Conner and Seth met in the conference room as well as Chief Kelly and a couple other agents working the case. Adrienne came in, too, but stayed as far away from the box as she could and yet still be in the room.

Donning latex gloves, Conner and Seth wasted no time in carefully opening the package. The outer packaging, as always, held nothing but the jeweler's box. Conner pulled the box out and set it on the table. Seth took the lid off the box.

It was all so horribly familiar. A single lock of hair. A typed note on a folded sheet of plain paper. No one spoke as Conner unfolded the paper and read it.

Simon says, you're still too slow.

There was no response. Everyone in the room knew

that the note meant another woman was dead. It would just be a matter of time until the body was discovered. Sometimes it was hours; sometimes it was days.

The packages were almost anticlimactic at this point. But still frustrating as hell.

Stepping back from the box, he realized everyone was looking at Adrienne. Only a select few were aware of the affect Conner had on Adrienne's abilities, so they obviously expected her to shed some sort of light on this newest arrival.

"Can I talk with you by my desk for a minute?" Conner asked Adrienne. She followed him out of the room. Seth wasn't far behind.

"I guess I'm going to go get some coffee." Conner grimaced. He knew he had to get away from the office in order for Adrienne to work. But he didn't like it.

Seth sighed dramatically. "Good. That should buy us some time. Since it takes twenty minutes for you to get out all the words in your order."

Conner ignored him as Adrienne put her hand on his arm. "I'm sorry. I know this has to be hard for you."

"I can take it as long as we catch this guy soon."

"You will." She squeezed his arm gently. "Don't go to the coffee shop in the lobby. You're still too close."

Conner rolled his eyes. "I know when I'm not wanted. I'm going. I'm going."

Adrienne released his arm. "But don't go far. I have a bad feeling about this one."

Conner nodded and left. Once outside he was overwhelmed with frustration again. There had to be something more he could do. Is this really what he had been reduced to at this point in his career—coffee boy?

This feeling of uselessness sucked. It went against everything in Conner's nature to sit on the sidelines while someone—*anyone*—else did the hard work. And knowing it was Adrienne suffering, and that he could stop it, left a bitter taste in his mouth. His every instinct was to protect her.

So, yes, Conner was pissed that he was four blocks away from his building getting coffee when Adrienne was back at the office fighting for her mental survival.

Conner gave his order to the cashier and paid. Yes, sugar-free vanilla in his latte. He couldn't tell if the ladies behind him were smirking at his order or not. Why did everyone find his drink choice so amusing?

Conner walked back outside. No matter how useless he felt, he was still glad he was able to help Adrienne. He didn't know why he blocked her powers, and he didn't care. He had no idea how she had survived her work with the FBI before.

Conner felt the phone buzz in his pocket, signaling a text message. It was too soon to hear from Seth or Adrienne; he'd only been gone about ten minutes. But the text was from Seth.

Come now.

Conner frowned at the phone. Another text appeared. *Hurry!*

The exclamation point had Conner dropping his drink in the nearby trash can and taking off at a dead run. If Seth was telling him to hurry, something was wrong.

Within minutes Conner was back at the building. The elevator was too slow in arriving so he bolted up the stairs, fear burning through his brain.

Conner tore into the conference room. Adrienne was lying on the ground, unconscious, blood dripping from both nostrils.

"What the hell? Seth, what happened?" Conner dropped on his knees beside her.

"Con, I have no idea. You left, and she got that pinched look like she always does. Then we came in here. She touched the box and went really still for a minute—that's not unusual. She said something about a hotel. Then she reached for the note, and it was like she had been electrocuted. She couldn't even get any words out. It looked like she was trying to scream, but there was no sound."

Conner checked Adrienne's pulse. It was thready and weak. There was no color to her face at all, causing the blood from her nose to stand out in the most garish way.

Seth continued, shaking his head. "Then she fell to the ground. It was like she was having some sort of seizure. I texted you immediately. Thank God you weren't far, man."

Conner continued to stare at Adrienne. Her breathing was not quite so shallow any longer, but she still wasn't waking up. He stroked her cheek gently.

"I think we should take her to the hospital," Conner said, looking up at Seth for the first time. Seth nodded.

"No," Adrienne's weak voice responded, and Conner jerked his gaze back to her. Her eyes didn't open. "I'll be okay in a minute. Just don't leave me." She felt blindly for Conner's hand with hers. Conner grabbed it and laced his fingers through hers.

"No, sweetheart. I won't leave you."

Seth ushered out the other people in the room and closed the door behind them. It seemed to Conner that some of Adrienne's color was returning. He felt her pulse again at her wrist. Stronger.

Seth came over with a tissue and handed it to Conner. Conner gently wiped the blood from her nose and applied a bit of pressure to stop the rest of the bleeding.

"Thanks," Adrienne whispered, opening her eyes.

"Hey." Conner smiled at her. "You know, if you want me to come back sooner, just ask. You don't have to go to all this drama."

Adrienne smiled at him. "Busted."

"You want to try to sit up or do you prefer lying down?"

"I think I'm okay to sit up. I'm feeling better."

Conner helped her, and they scooted over until they were leaning back against the couch with their legs stretched out in front of them. Seth sat in a chair at the table.

"So, that was not awesome," Adrienne finally said.

"What the hell happened, Adrienne?" Seth asked. "That was worse than anything I've seen."

"Believe me, it was worse than anything I've *felt*." Conner was close enough to feel her shudder. "The feeling was so strong. It was like he was in the room with us. He was laughing this horrible mocking laugh."

Adrienne drew her knees up to her chest and wrapped her arms around her legs. "And then he reached out to touch me, and I just lost it. I felt like my body was burning. I was screaming."

"It looked like you were trying to scream," Seth corrected her. "But no sound came out of your mouth."

"I don't know why I had such a huge reaction. Maybe because he touched it so recently? I don't know. Maybe that's why the feelings are so strong."

There was a brief knock on the conference room door. An agent stuck his head in.

"There's been a call, guys. Woman's body found at

a hotel on Harrison Street. Locals called it in. Pretty sure it's Simon."

Seth looked at Adrienne. "You said something about a hotel before you fell."

Adrienne nodded and looked up sadly. "Yes. It's definitely her. Simon's latest victim."

ADRIENNE WAS EXHAUSTED. Riding in the backseat of the car with Conner and Seth on the way to the crime scene, she could admit the exhaustion to herself, even if she didn't want to admit it to anyone else.

She knew the guys weren't exactly happy she was with them, but what else could they do? Either Conner had to stay at the field office with her—and there was no way in hell that was happening—or she had to come with him. Adrienne didn't really want to see the crime scene. After what had happened this morning, she just wanted to get far away from all of humanity, go to bed, pull the covers over her head and sleep for a week.

This morning had scared her. The only time she'd ever had a reaction that strong was when the perpetrator had been in close proximity and had turned his malice toward her. It was like Simon had *known* she was there. But Adrienne knew that couldn't be right, because she would've felt him long before touching the letter.

There was something not normal about this serial killer. Adrienne just didn't know what it was yet. *A not-normal serial killer. Go figure.* Adrienne barely refrained from scoffing at herself out loud.

They pulled up outside the motel where the body had been found. This was definitely the place she had seen in her vision.

"Do you want us to clear the scene so you can go in first?" Conner asked.

She knew how hard that question was for him. Clearing the scene would include clearing him also. She couldn't imagine that option sat well with him.

"No. If it's okay with you guys, I just want to sit here for a while. The other people being in there won't make any difference for me." She saw relief flutter across Conner's face before he hurried out of the car.

She watched all the activity for a long while—a crime scene was a busy place. Technicians, photographers, local law enforcement buzzed around everywhere. It wouldn't be long before the press was here, and the bystanders. Local officers were already roping off a good area of the scene so it wouldn't be disturbed. Adrienne watched it all with interest. It was actually the first crime scene she had been at where she could just observe like a normal person. Until Conner left, Adrienne's abilities wouldn't work. Blessed silence.

The entire place would be photographed then fingerprinted. The room and body would be scoured for forensic evidence. Adrienne doubted they would find any. Simon had proved to be quite fastidious so far about not leaving any evidence behind.

Eventually, a tall, lanky man, camera clutched in his hand, came up to the car. He tapped on Adrienne's window and smiled. Adrienne opened her door.

"Hi, Ms. Jeffries. I'm Victor Faraday, FBI photographer. It's nice to meet you." The man spoke rapidly, in a much higher pitch than Adrienne would expect from someone his size. "Can I get you anything? Are you okay?"

The photographer—she'd already forgotten his name—was definitely odd, but seemed sincere in wanting to assist Adrienne. She smiled distractedly at him. "I'm fine. Thanks. Just waiting."

"Okay. Agent Perigo sent me to tell you that you can come in. We're done with photography, and I believe the forensics team is finished also."

Adrienne thanked the man and got out of the car. She walked slowly up to the hotel room door. Looking at the photos over the past few days had been bad enough; she was not looking forward to seeing the crime scene live.

Conner saw her and came over.

"Already in here? I thought you were going to wait for me to get you. You okay?"

Adrienne ignored his comment about not waiting for him. She had waited until he'd sent Victor out, right? She hugged her arms around herself. "Not really. I have to be honest. I'm not looking forward to this."

Conner reached over and rubbed her upper arms and hands. Adrienne couldn't help but lean a little toward his strength. "Give me about five minutes, and I'll get out of here."

Adrienne nodded. Might as well get it over with. She glanced around the room, purposely avoiding looking at the body on the bed, and waited. It wasn't long before Conner returned.

"Seth and I have worked out a plan. I'm going to go a couple blocks away in the car, so I can get back here immediately if needed. I'll be on the phone the entire time with Seth, so as soon as I'm far enough for you to start getting clear feelings, let him know."

Adrienne was touched that they had taken time to figure out how to best balance the needs of the case with her well-being. She smiled at Conner then stood on tiptoe quickly and kissed his cheek.

"Thank you."

Conner winked at her and strode out the door. A

few moments later she heard the car starting and pulling away.

It didn't take long for Conner to be far enough away for Adrienne's abilities to work.

"Tell him to go just a little farther, Seth, then stop. I'm getting stuff now."

Seth relayed the message to Conner on his phone then turned back to Adrienne. "Are you okay? My heart cannot stand another repeat of this morning."

Adrienne took deep calming breaths to focus herself. "I think I'm okay. I'm just going to take it slow."

For the first time Adrienne looked over at the dead woman lying on the bed. She walked over to her. Obviously, like the other victims, this woman had been stabbed to death. Adrienne touched her ankle featherlight.

Boring. This one was not nearly as fun as the others. She just cried quietly. Killing the last one had brought such a high because she had been so bossy and bad. Killing her had been fun. But this one was pathetic.

As soon as Adrienne removed her hand from the woman's leg, the killer's thoughts stopped. She looked over at Seth, who was furiously writing in his notebook.

"Anything else?" he asked.

"Was I saying that out loud?"

"Yeah. About him being bored and stuff. I'm just trying to get it all down." He pointed to the phone, now on speaker-mode, on the table next to him. "Conner is listening, also."

Adrienne touched the dead woman's ankle lightly again. She didn't want to go anywhere near the stab wounds at the top of the woman's body.

She couldn't breathe right, so of course she couldn't scream. The screaming was what made it fun.

Adrienne let go of the woman's ankle. She knew what happened next. He killed her. Adrienne didn't want to see that.

She looked over at Seth. "She had asthma or something. She couldn't scream, so it wasn't as fulfilling for him."

Seth nodded. "Anything else?"

Adrienne walked around the room but couldn't seem to get any reading. She decided to experiment. "Tell Conner to drive away a little farther. I can't hear anything right now except from the body. Maybe if he's not so close, I'll be able to get something else."

Seth relayed the message to Conner, and Adrienne walked around the room some more. But still nothing. "He's very careful, methodical, when he's placing the bodies. Not angry. It's difficult for me to get any information."

The general buzzing got louder, and Adrienne's head began pounding, and her stomach rolled, so she knew Conner was far enough away not to affect her. She touched different pieces of furniture in the room, hoping to pick up something from them, but had no luck. She was giving up and about to leave when the image came to her.

"Seth! He was standing right over here in this corner." Adrienne rushed over there and placed herself where she saw the killer. "Watching. Almost like he was watching while you were in here processing the scene. He knew or envisioned or *something* what it would be like when you all got here and found the body."

Adrienne followed the actions of the killer in her mind. "He laughed to think of you here, unable to figure anything out. Then he turned and walked out the door."

Adrienne followed the same path outside, knowing

Seth was right behind her. "He turned and walked down this block to where his car was parked. He knew not to park it in front of the hotel. He had to hurry. There was something he wanted to see, to make sure he didn't miss."

"Miss what?" Seth asked.

"I don't know. He keeps thinking of it as 'the show.'"

Adrienne stopped and looked down. "He dropped his keys here, and he was mad. He was going to miss the show if he didn't hurry."

Adrienne stopped and looked around, confused.

"What happened then?" Seth asked.

"I don't know. He just disappeared."

"You mean he got into his car?"

"No. He reached down to get his keys. And then I couldn't see him anymore." Adrienne rubbed her forehead. Why had she lost him like that? There were no other people around, nothing to confuse her. She shouldn't have lost him like that.

"He was just gone," Adrienne explained to Seth. "I don't know why. It doesn't happen like that."

She looked around but didn't pick up any other images from the killer. "Conner didn't come back, did he?" But she knew he hadn't, because her head still hurt and she could hear all the buzzing. So what was the problem?

Seth was about to double check with Conner when Adrienne interrupted him. "Never mind. You can tell him to come back. I can't see anything else here."

Adrienne walked back to the crime scene, frustrated. She was frustrated with herself, with what had happened, with why she couldn't get a clear, full glimpse into the killer's mind. Was it her that was the problem? Was it Conner?

It brought her back to her thought from earlier today: she was dealing with something *not normal*. Well, she better figure out what that *not normal* was before another woman died.

Conner returned a few minutes later and walked directly over to Adrienne. "You okay?"

"Yes. Just tired. This is all so strange, so different from other cases I've worked. I'm frustrated."

"I know you are. Let Seth and I finish up here, and I'll take you back to the hotel."

Adrienne nodded and got back into Conner's car to wait for them to process the scene. A lot of work, a lot of people to manage and, as the agents in charge, everyone kept coming to Conner and Seth for answers and instructions. Adrienne didn't mind waiting in the relatively peaceful cocoon of the car. At some point one of the local police officers even brought her a sandwich, which she ate gratefully.

Eventually everything wrapped up, and Conner and Seth were ready to leave the scene. She saw them chat for a moment before Conner came to the car and Seth headed in the other direction.

"Seth is going to get a ride back to the office so I can take you straight to the hotel. I know you're exhausted. Sorry it took so long." Conner started the car and pulled out into the street.

"That's all right. It was interesting watching everyone work."

"Yeah, the locals have been pretty great about working with us in this case. That doesn't always happen. Cops can get pretty territorial about their cases. I think we all just want to catch this son of a bitch."

"Me, too." Adrienne sighed.

Conner reached over and took her hand. "You're

doing your best, Adrienne. Seth told me about today. You can't let that upset you. Everything you've done has helped, and we're all grateful."

"But it hasn't been enough!" Adrienne's frustration burst from her.

"It will be. We'll get ahead of him."

Exhaustion poured over Adrienne. She was tired of killers and dead bodies and voices and visions of evil in her head. She just wanted one night of good solid sleep with no buzzing or static to keep waking her.

They pulled up to her hotel. Conner parked the car and came around to open her door. "You're dead on your feet." He trailed a finger down her cheek. Adrienne could feel the warmth it left behind. "These days are rough on you, I know."

"The nights aren't great, either."

Conner grimaced. "No wonder you're tired all the time. Trouble sleeping?"

"Every night. Seems to be getting worse."

Conner put a hand at the small of her back and led her inside the hotel. "I'll stay here tonight. In the lobby. That should give you a peaceful night's sleep."

Adrienne wasn't sure how to respond. She was so grateful for his offer. The thought of having a night of uninterrupted rest made her feel like a huge weight had been lifted from her shoulders.

But she didn't want him in the lobby. She wanted him in her bed.

Adrienne smiled up at Conner shyly and reached for his hand. "There's no need for you to stay down here."

He pressed the button for the elevator then stepped close enough to Adrienne that his lips were just inches away from hers.

"I think we both know if I stay up there, a peaceful night's sleep is not what's going to happen."

The elevator door opened, but Conner didn't move. Finally Adrienne put a finger on his chest and pushed him into the elevator and didn't stop until Conner's back was against the elevator's wall. The doors closed behind them.

"Sleeping is overrated." Adrienne reached up and threaded her hands through his hair, bringing his lips down to hers.

She pulled Conner's lips to hers in a fierce kiss. She could feel a moment's hesitation before he gave himself fully over to the passion between them. Adrienne gasped as Conner spun her around so her back was against the wall. He wrapped his arms around her hips and lifted her so they were eye to eye.

Heat pooled in her belly as he pressed up against her. She hooked one elbow around the back of his neck to pull him closer, deepening the kiss. He groaned, rocking against her, setting off sparks of electricity up and down her spine.

Adrienne vaguely heard the elevator door *bing* and open—she couldn't remember either of them even pushing her floor's button. Conner groaned and slid her slowly down his body and onto her feet. Then trailed his hands up from her hips past her waist to her shoulders, then cupped her cheeks.

He grabbed her hand and led her from the elevator to her room. Adrienne found the card key in her purse and handed it to Conner, who unlocked the door. He jerked her to him as he opened the door, and Adrienne giggled. Her giggling stopped when his mouth captured hers again, closing the door behind him with his foot.

After a moment, Adrienne eased away from Conner

and turned to put her purse on the table, flipping on the light. Her breath came in a shocked gasp as she turned and looked around her.

Her hotel room was in shambles. Someone had destroyed nearly everything in it.

Chapter Eleven

When Conner heard Adrienne's shocked gasp he immediately threw her behind his body and drew his weapon. The room was completely destroyed. He checked under the bed, in the closet and bathroom, cursing himself for not securing the room when he had first walked in, but found nothing.

Conner saw Adrienne still looking around with huge eyes, trying to take it all in. An envelope on the pillow—the one area of the room not destroyed—caught her attention. Before he could stop her, she walked over to the bed to read the note.

When she saw what it said, her hands began to shake.

"Conner?" Her voice came out as a hoarse whisper. He was immediately at her side and took the note from her.

Simon says, don't worry, it's almost your turn.

Conner lowered Adrienne's shaking form to the bed. He immediately called Seth.

"Seth. I'm at the hotel with Adrienne. Simon Says has been here. He ransacked the room, left a note on her bed." Conner glanced over at Adrienne, glad she couldn't hear the expletives that came out of Seth's mouth when he understood the full ramifications of the situation. "I need you to get the full team up here right away."

Conner turned back to where Adrienne still sat on the bed. She didn't seem to have moved from where he had placed her. The letter was still gripped in her shaking hands, but she wasn't looking at it. Her eyes were unfocused, staring at some faraway place only she could see.

"Hey, sweetheart," Conner said gently, kneeling in front of her perch on the bed. "Adrienne?"

She finally focused in on him. His heart broke as big tears filled her eyes then spilled onto her cheeks.

"He was here, Conner. In my room."

Conner caught her tears with his fingers. "I know, baby."

"How long ago? How did he get in here? How did he know where to find me? And what could he be looking for?" She stood up as her panic built. Conner stood with her. She grabbed the front of his shirt. "Do you think he's still around here?"

Conner was reminded that Adrienne wasn't a trained FBI agent. Just a young woman who had seen way too much violence in her lifetime. Now the psychopath had turned his madness toward her. She was rightfully panicked.

He covered the hand that gripped his shirt and rubbed it gently. "Adrienne, no, he's not here. I already checked the room and the hallway. There's nobody around."

She nodded up at him weakly.

"Seth and the team are on their way. We should try not to touch anything until they process the scene."

Adrienne released his shirt and stood. She looked around the room like she'd never seen it before, then turned back to him. "Maybe you should leave and I'll… see what I can see."

Conner immediately closed the space between them. He gripped her upper arms. "There is no way in hell I'm leaving you here alone. You got that? Don't even say it." He would not leave her now.

"But…"

Conner put his hands on both sides of her face and stroked her cheeks with this thumbs. "Baby, no. I'm not leaving you."

Intense relief flashed through Adrienne's eyes. She had been willing to try, Conner realized—and appreciated—but she would've paid a high price for it.

Conner led Adrienne out of the room and down to the lobby. He explained to the night manager that there had been a break-in and that an FBI team was coming to process the scene. Finding out that the room next to Adrienne's was available, he asked for the keys to it. Adrienne could stay there while they processed her room.

Conner would not leave Adrienne alone in this hotel. In any hotel. Not now. He would take her home with him. She would stay there until they caught Simon Says.

It wasn't long before Seth and the rest of the team arrived. Adrienne still had that exhausted, pinched look about her and gave no fight when Conner suggested she stay in the room next door. Conner posted one of the agents as a guard at the door, just to be safe.

Seth looked as ticked as Conner when he saw the room and the note. Conner's anger increased even more as he saw how Adrienne's clothes had been ripped into pieces and thrown all over the room.

Deliberate, ugly violence.

"Thank God you were with her, man," Seth said through clenched teeth.

Conner could barely stand to think about the alternative. "What if I hadn't been, Seth? What if I had just dropped her off, and she had discovered this alone?"

Something like this would be scary enough for any woman to walk in on. But who knows how it would've affected Adrienne. Simon having been in her room? Having touched everything around her? A note directed especially to her?

Conner remembered Adrienne's reaction this morning to Simon's latest package. It had knocked her out cold. Almost had them taking her to the hospital.

What would've happened to her if Conner wasn't around to block it and there was no one there to help her get out of the room?

Conner didn't even want to think about it. He was filled with the overwhelming urge to get Adrienne out of here—away from the violence that had bombarded her all day.

"Seth, Adrienne can't deal with anything right now. I'm taking her to my place. Bag everything, and she'll look at it when she's ready."

Seth nodded, and Conner was grateful not to get any flak from his partner. Conner went to the next room to get Adrienne and found her in the same seat where he'd left her, looking off into space.

He walked up to her slowly, careful not to startle her. He sat down in the chair beside her and gently touched her arm. She blinked and looked over at him.

"Hey," she whispered.

"You ready to go?"

Adrienne nodded and stood up.

"I'm going to take you to my place. I have a town house in Daly City, not too far from here."

Adrienne nodded again, then rubbed her hands up and down her arms as if to warm herself.

"Cold?"

"Yeah. But my jacket was…" She swallowed hard and shrugged.

Conner took off his blazer, slipped it around her shoulders and watched her snuggle into its warmth. Not having his jacket meant his holster and weapon showed, but Conner didn't care. He got Adrienne downstairs and bundled into his car. Her huge eyes peering at him still looked overwhelmed.

The drive to Daly City—a suburb of San Francisco—didn't take long at this time of the evening. Conner tried to talk to Adrienne about neutral things, like his family, who lived in Nevada, and how he had inherited this town house from his grandmother, the only way he could possibly afford a place like this anywhere near San Fran on his salary.

Adrienne didn't say much, but she seemed to listen.

They parked at the town house, and Conner helped her out of his car and in his front door. Her eyes still held that somewhat vacant look. He wished she would cry or yell or anything but keep what she was feeling buried inside her.

"How about some hot tea?" he asked as he herded her into the kitchen and sat her down by the table.

"Chai tea?"

"If that's what you want. Sure."

"Only if it's sugar-free vanilla and has no foam." A ghost of a smile passed her lips.

Conner was relieved to see even that tiny smile. "Smart aleck."

"So this is where you live?"

"Yep. For about six years now."

"Always been just you?"

"Is that a more subtle way of asking if I've ever been married?" Conner chuckled when Adrienne blushed. "I lived here with my grandmother for a couple years before she died. But since then, it's just been me."

"Mind if I look around?"

Conner was glad some life was returning to Adrienne. "Sure, be my guest. But please excuse any mess. I wasn't expecting company."

Adrienne wandered around looking at his pictures and knickknacks. A lot of it was decorations from before his grandmother had passed away. Conner had just never changed it.

"How about you?" he asked as he finished making their tea. "Ever married?"

"No. After my work with the FBI before, I just needed to totally be away from people for a while. Then I never found the right guy, I guess."

"Not a whole lot of guys in Lodi. How'd you end up there?"

"That's where my foster mother's family was from. She had passed away and left me some money, plus I saved a lot while I worked for the Bureau, since I never had any free time. It ended up being enough for the down payment on the horse ranch."

"You love horses?"

"I love how they don't put any voices or thoughts into my head, mostly. But I've grown to love them, yeah."

Conner smiled and walked over, handing Adrienne the mug of tea.

"How did you end up working with the Bureau anyway?" Conner sat down in his normal recliner across from the couch. But Adrienne seemed more interested in walking around, looking at things: his pictures, his books, his DVDs.

"I was eighteen. After my foster mother—really the only person I called family—died, I had to go into San Francisco for some business with her will at the courthouse. As you can imagine, a courthouse is not the best place for me to be with my gift."

Conner could imagine.

"Plus I was used to living in a small town," Adrienne continued, still wandering around his living room looking at things. "I was a mess, hardly able to function. I literally ran into Chief Kelly, knocking all the papers out of his briefcase. I went to hand a photo back to him—it was a picture of one of the Bureau's 'most wanted' criminals—and got a clear image of exactly where the guy was right at that moment. Which happened to be just a couple blocks away as he was about to rob a convenience store."

Adrienne came and sat down on the couch across from Conner's chair.

"And?"

She smiled. "Well, I told him what I saw. I have to give Chief Kelly credit—he didn't laugh or scoff or arrest me. He called it in, and they caught him. Right where I said he'd be.

"After careful vetting and making sure I wasn't that guy's accomplice, Kelly offered me a job as a 'consultant.'" She sighed. "I was eighteen and had nobody. I wanted to do something important. To make a difference."

"You did make a difference, Adrienne. You still are making a difference."

Adrienne shrugged. "I guess. Part of me always felt

like I was a coward for quitting. Even though I honestly had no alternative at the time. It was too much."

Conner came and sat next to Adrienne on the couch. "I've seen the price you pay for using your talents, Adrienne. Nobody should've expected you to keep paying that price. It couldn't be done. And you were a *teenager,* for heaven's sake."

Adrienne leaned her head back against the top of the couch. "My perspective on that time has changed, thanks to you."

"What do you mean?"

"I now understand what my job with the FBI could've been like, if it had been done right. You've shown me how much more I can handle if I can just get some sort of rest and reprieve in between."

Conner sighed. "I don't know how true that is. You're still exhausted and in pain a lot of the time."

"Yeah, but I know there is a time coming every day when I won't be in pain. When there won't be noise. That's thanks to you."

"I wish I could've been around ten years ago."

"That would've been ideal." Adrienne turned her face toward him and grinned without lifting her head from the couch. "But I realize now, if I had just demanded time off in between cases to recuperate—that would've made a huge difference. And I needed to get a place out of town so I wasn't always bombarded by noise in my time off."

"You were eighteen. Most eighteen-year-olds are trying to figure out which English class to take at college or how to get beer without being carded."

Adrienne shrugged. "Yeah? Is that what you were like at eighteen?"

"Pretty much. I always knew I wanted to be in law

enforcement, so I stayed pretty clean. Went into the Bureau right out of college."

"Never married?"

"No. Engaged once, back East. But she really wasn't interested in the hours an agent has to put in. Glad we figured it out before we got married. No harm, no foul."

Adrienne reached for his mug and took it along with hers back to the kitchen. Conner could hear the water running as she rinsed them out.

"It's still pretty early," he called out to her. "Want to watch some TV?"

Adrienne returned from the kitchen and stopped right in front of Conner on the couch. "No, actually what I was hoping is that you might kiss me some more, and we could eventually work our way to you showing me your bedroom."

ADRIENNE WASN'T SURE she had ever wanted anyone as much as she wanted Conner Perigo right now. Glancing down at him, she could see myriad emotions cross his face: concern, hesitation, passion. He was worried about her vulnerable state. He didn't want to take advantage. She truly appreciated that he was the type of man who would consider these things and want to do what was right.

But she wasn't going to allow it to get in her way tonight.

Adrienne could admit she had been shaken earlier. What she saw in her hotel room had frightened her. Deeply. And she knew she was going to have to deal with it and process it—but not right now. Here in this house, enveloped by all the items Conner held dear— pictures, knickknacks, items of the past and the present—Adrienne felt safe. This was a house centered in love and security. Adrienne could feel herself drawing strength from it.

They had right now. Adrienne wasn't going to waste it. Vicious psycho on their radar or not, nobody ever knew how many tomorrows they had.

Conner still hadn't responded. He was eyeing her warily, as if he couldn't quite decide the best way to talk her down from this particular ledge.

Obviously he was going to need a little help getting over his nobility.

Adrienne crossed the few remaining steps to him. She leaned down to where he sat on the couch and put her hands on his knees. She smiled at him.

"Adrienne…"

Adrienne leaned the rest of the way and kissed him. Lightly. She put her hands on his shoulders. He didn't pull away, but he didn't pull her to him, either.

"I'm not sure this is a good idea." Conner rested his forehead against hers.

"You may be right," Adrienne said, smiling again. "But I don't think we have enough data collected yet to be sure."

Not giving him a chance to respond, Adrienne straddled her legs on either side of his on the couch and lowered herself the rest of the way onto his lap. She took his face between her hands and kissed him.

Adrienne kissed him with all the passion she'd felt for him since the moment she'd met him.

It didn't take long for Conner to give up the fight. She heard him sigh as his arms hooked around her hips, pulling her closer to him. Everything about them seemed to explode. The hot, needful pressure of his mouth made her dizzy. Her hands locked in fistfuls of his hair as he released her lips and began kissing his way along her jaw to her throat. His mouth slid to the soft hollow beneath her ear, placing a not-too-gentle bite on that side of her neck.

Adrienne felt the heat inside her intensify. She whispered his name and dragged his mouth back to hers, drowning in the kiss. She reached between them and unbuttoned his shirt, loving the feel of his chest against her palms. She felt him reach for the hem of her T-shirt and broke their kiss long enough for him to peel it over her head.

Conner's lips returned to her neck, nipping with just enough force to drive her absolutely crazy. His hands unhooked and removed her bra, then cupped her breasts.

"You're beautiful."

Adrienne could hear the reverence in Conner's tone as he kissed her again. She wrapped her fingers in his hair and held him to her.

Abruptly Conner pried her off him and stood, wasting no time getting the rest of her clothes off her. He made quick work of his own, then reached under her hips with both arms and lifted her again. She wrapped her arms around his neck and her legs around his waist. He carried her up the stairs.

"You mentioned something about wanting to see my bedroom?" He raised one eyebrow.

Adrienne giggled. "So considerate of you to give me the tour."

"We aim to please."

His bedroom was decidedly masculine with heavy wooden furniture. A plain cream-colored duvet was thrown haphazardly across the bed—as if he had attempted to make it up this morning, but hadn't been willing to give it more than thirty seconds' worth of effort. Conner tossed the cover to the side and eased

Adrienne onto the bed and followed down right on top of her.

His lips found hers again, and Adrienne gave herself over to the feeling of being utterly surrounded by Conner. Being held against him felt good. His incredible body heat felt good. Everything about this felt good. With every touch he aroused another wave of sensation.

For the first time ever, Adrienne gave herself over to passion without holding back, knowing without a doubt she was safe.

THE NEXT MORNING Conner looked over at Adrienne asleep in his bed. She was curled around a pillow, tucked up in a tiny ball. Her deep, even breathing suggested she was a long way from waking up. Good, she needed sleep. Last night had been wonderful, but it definitely had not helped her get any rest. Conner couldn't bring himself to be sorry about that.

He had wanted her like he'd never wanted another woman. It was all he could do now to just leave her alone.

Conner eased himself from the bed, careful not to disturb her. He grabbed some sweatpants from out of a drawer and put them on as he headed downstairs to the coffeemaker.

Yeah, Conner was glad Adrienne was asleep. She was going to need it now that it seemed Simon Says had turned his sights on her.

The thought made Conner break out in a cold sweat. Simon knew who Adrienne was, had known where she was staying. And they still knew next to nothing about him.

Conner made coffee—a full pot; he was going to

need it—and sat down at his kitchen table. His phone chirped from the counter. A text from Seth.

You up?

Conner texted him back, Yeah.

There in five. Bringing breakfast.

Conner was always up for a delivered meal but was especially glad Seth was coming over. It would give them a chance to talk through the thought that had come to Conner sometime in the night.

Simon Says was an FBI agent. Or a cop. Or some sort of law enforcement.

It was the only way he could've known who Adrienne was or that she was working with them.

It hadn't occurred to Conner while they were processing Adrienne's room at the hotel, probably because he had been too caught up with getting Adrienne out of there as soon as possible. But now that he had thought about it, it was the only thing that made sense.

There was a tap on the door, and Conner got up to answer it. Seth walked through, thrusting a bag of breakfast sandwiches at Conner.

"Simon Says is a cop," Seth said with no preamble.

Conner didn't need one. "I agree. I was just thinking that myself. A cop or agent. Some sort of law enforcement."

They sat down at the kitchen table and opened the sandwiches. "We've worked with a lot of people over the past six months. It could be any of them." Seth looked at the sandwich he got and traded it with Conner. "But it at least gives us a place to start looking. A way to narrow things down."

Conner took a bite of his breakfast. "It can't be someone at the Bureau office. Adrienne would be totally incapacitated just by him being around."

"Unless you're there blocking everything," Seth pointed out.

"Yeah, but how could he know that? We haven't told anybody. That would be taking an awfully big risk."

"Well, obviously this guy doesn't have a problem taking risks."

"I want her with one of us all the time, Seth. Or at least always in the Bureau office." Conner set his sandwich down and sat back in his chair shaking his head. "If Simon got her alone— You've seen what she's like after accessing evidence. Could you imagine how helpless she'd be if Simon actually got his hands on her?"

Conner was determined not to let that happen.

"We could get a protection detail on her."

Conner shook his head. "No. Not until we know for sure who we can trust. It could be anyone."

"Who could be anyone?" Adrienne's voice came softly from behind them over at the stairs.

Conner turned to her and was immediately stunned at how beautiful she was despite being in one of his T-shirts and a pair of his shorts. Or maybe she was so gorgeous because she was in them, even though they were huge on her.

Whichever. He had it bad.

"Good morning." Conner smiled at her. "Want some coffee?"

"Yeah, I'll get it. Hi, Seth."

"Morning, Adrienne."

Adrienne walked into the kitchen. Conner turned

back in his seat to find Seth looking at him with one eyebrow cocked.

"Shut up. I don't want to hear it," Conner muttered.

"And to think I was just about to comment on how gentlemanly of you it was to have taken the couch and let her sleep in your bed."

"Things just worked out differently."

"I'm just kidding you, man. The way you two have been from the very beginning, I'm surprised it has taken this long."

Adrienne walked back in, saving Conner from needing to reply. She came to stand next to him and he looped his arm around her waist, pulling her down into his lap. Without any thought to Seth whatsoever, he kissed her thoroughly.

"Good morning to you, too," Adrienne said, blushing, when Conner finally released her mouth. "What are you guys talking about?"

Conner was loath to bring it up but knew Adrienne should know. They explained their theory about Simon Says being in law enforcement. Listening, Adrienne got more and more tense in his lap.

"We want one of us to be with you, or you to be at the Bureau office all the time," Conner concluded.

Adrienne stood up. "That's not going to work. I'm going to need to go back to the ranch soon, at least for a few days. Vince can't run everything there alone forever."

Conner shook his head again. "No, Adrienne, you can't go back there right now. Not until we've caught Simon."

"But that could take months!"

Conner could feel his frustration building. She could not leave—he wouldn't allow it. He wouldn't let anything compromise her safety. "It won't take months. Not with you helping us." Conner reached out to Adrienne, but she stepped back from his grasp. Conner looked over at Seth, but found his partner was looking down at his hands, unwilling to get involved.

"Conner, I will take normal, reasonable precautions. Of course I don't want Simon to get ahold of me. But my abilities allow me to know if he's nearby, so I don't have to worry about that."

Conner couldn't think of a logical argument against what Adrienne was saying. "Three days. Give us three days to narrow down the pool of suspects. During that time, you stay with one of us or in the middle of the Bureau office. After three days we can reevaluate."

Conner watched as Adrienne considered his offer. She didn't like to be boxed into a decision, he could tell. Finally she nodded her head. He reached out for her again, and she took his extended hand.

"Okay. Three days."

Chapter Twelve

The three days were tough. Conner watched as Adrienne worked herself into exhaustion trying to help them. She fleshed out details about Simon Says—his thoughts, his motives—and the crimes. Based on comparing how tall the victims were with what angle Simon held his head while looking at them, Adrienne determined roughly how tall the killer was—around five foot ten.

She worked with an artist to provide a rendering of the room where the women were killed. And went through file after file, package after package, to see what insight she could gather. With the information Adrienne provided, both Conner and Seth knew they would eventually gain the upper hand on Simon.

What Adrienne could do—her freakishly awesome crime-fighting superpowers—was truly amazing. And the price she paid for it was hideous. Of course Conner always saw both secondhand. He had pretty much been banned from the office while Adrienne was working. He spent a lot of time around the city, going back over crime scenes, reinterviewing different parties, trying to piece together anything they may have missed the first time. He didn't like being away from Adrienne—not when Simon could be anyone at the Bureau.

But in order for them to get ahead in the case Conner had to stay away. Each afternoon he would return to the office and watch the footage of what happened with Adrienne while he was gone. He watched as she pored over any item they had associated with the murder and gleaned whatever information she could. And the cost she paid to do it.

Watching Adrienne go through such mental torture on a daily basis—knowing he could stop it at any time—was destroying Conner. He was torn between wanting to catch a sadistic killer and protecting the woman he loved.

The woman he loved?

Where exactly had that come from? Conner shrugged, didn't fight it. In the short time he had known Adrienne, she had eased her way into his heart. And he wanted her there. The moment he'd seen her walking into that barn last week, talking about some crazy horse, that had been it for him.

Of course, he had no idea how Adrienne felt. And he couldn't imagine why she would ever want to stay in San Francisco or ever be a part of the Bureau. The price she paid was too high.

Conner tried to be a buffer for her as much as possible, but it wasn't easy. Not only did she have the Simon Says case to work on, but soon word had gotten out around the building that the Bloodhound was real, not an urban legend. That she was back. That she was here. Everybody wanted to meet her or shake her hand or just ask for a moment's worth of help.

It was like Adrienne could spin straw into gold, and everyone wanted to bring their little bit of straw to her.

Not that any of the other agents meant any harm. At worst, they were just overly curious. At best, they wanted insight on a case or two so they could help justice prevail.

Not unlike him and Seth.

The problem was, nobody realized the price Adrienne paid for the help she gave. The violence and malice she was exposed to whenever she touched something new to help someone's case. The pain and exhaustion that often overwhelmed her.

Because Adrienne never told anyone it hurt. Someone would ask for her help, and she would do it. They would have all sorts of curious questions about her abilities, and she would answer with some light joke— putting them at ease. As far as he could tell from the footage he had watched, her favorite responses for when she was asked how she got her abilities were radioactive spider bite, bombardment of cosmic rays and gamma-radiation accident—all comic book characters' plights if Conner wasn't mistaken.

Conner wasn't sure how she functioned so efficiently or how she was able to keep such an upbeat personality when she was pelted all day by malice of the worst kind. But somehow she did.

The nights were better. Adrienne had moved in with him for all intents and purposes. Only Conner, Seth and Chief Kelly knew Adrienne's location. Until they discovered who Simon was, Conner intended to keep it that way.

They spent their evenings together with quiet dinners and walks around the city. He loved how the tension that surrounded her when he arrived at the office each afternoon was gone by the end of the evening. He was glad to offer her peace and quiet. And relieved to have her in his bed every night, knowing she was safe and not in any pain.

But having to be away from the office—away from the action—during the day was frustrating as hell.

Conner was gone now as Adrienne prepared to go through her own ruined clothes from the hotel. Simon had shredded most of them into pieces. Because it was her own stuff, this would probably be worse for Adrienne. So Conner didn't want to go far. In the past few days they had worked out exactly how many blocks away he needed to be in order for Adrienne's abilities to work.

One of the FBI photographers, Victor Faraday, had seemed to figure out what was going on with Conner and Adrienne, or at least that Conner was never in the room when Adrienne was using her abilities, and had shown Conner how to set up a video chat on his phone so he could see what was happening, even if he wasn't there. They were trying that now.

That made it easier, but not much.

"Okay, Seth, I'm far enough out, I think," Conner told Seth, looking into his phone.

"Okay. Faraday is going to hold the camera so I can help Adrienne if she needs it. She's opening the first of the crime scene bags now." The camera zoomed in on Adrienne and the bags.

Conner didn't like how pale she already was. Before even touching her clothes.

Adrienne cut open one of the crime scene bags and reached inside for what looked like had once been a sweater. He saw Adrienne tense as she touched it, but she didn't say anything.

"Adrienne?" Seth placed his hand on her arm. Adrienne shook her head but didn't answer. Instead she reached for a different bag, pulling out its contents. She spread her fingers wide over them so she could touch as much as possible.

"Seth, am I missing something? What's going on? Faraday, do we have audio?" Conner asked.

Victor Faraday was the one who answered. "Ms. Jeffries isn't saying anything, Agent Perigo. The audio is fine."

Adrienne tore a third evidence bag open more quickly than she had the first two. She pulled out their contents, careful to touch every piece. But still she said nothing. Conner waited as she did the same to the other three bags.

"Conner?" Adrienne finally looked over at the camera Faraday was holding.

"What, sweetheart?" The endearment was out before he could catch it. Conner supposed it didn't matter— Seth already knew, and Faraday wasn't high enough on the Bureau food chain to really matter. Although hopefully he wouldn't say anything.

"There's nothing, Conner," Adrienne responded.

"Do you think I'm too close? Is that it?"

"No. I can feel Simon on the clothes. He definitely had some sort of plan and was in the room. But when he did all this damage, he was not in any rage. At least none that I would be able to feel."

"What do you think that means?"

He saw Adrienne shake her head. "I don't know. He wasn't menacing in any way while he was destroying the room. So it's really hard for me to get any reading from any of this."

"Are you positive it was Simon?" Seth asked.

"Definitely. He just wasn't angry when he did this.

Had no malicious intent toward me or anyone. It's like he was doing a job, calmly and methodically."

Conner's eyes narrowed. "Calmly and methodically" scared him almost more than "murderous rage."

"I can't see anything else. I'm sorry." Adrienne sighed.

"Don't worry about it. I'm coming back."

ADRIENNE WASN'T SURE what to make of this. It all just wasn't right—as if Simon knew the weakness in her visions and was exploiting them. Without malicious intent on the killer's part, she really couldn't see anything clearly.

But only someone who knew the type of work she did for the FBI would know that. Adrienne was becoming more and more convinced of Conner's theory that whoever Simon was, he had some sort of link to law enforcement in this area.

From where she sat at Conner's desk, Adrienne looked around. There were people everywhere in this building—agents, suspects, witnesses. Most of them she didn't know at all.

Any of them could be the killer.

Adrienne shook her head and chased away that thought. No, Simon Says couldn't be in this building. If he was, Adrienne would know it. Even now she could hear the buzz of everyone around her and feel some of the malevolent thoughts and artifacts pushing their way toward her. There was no way a killer could slip by her unnoticed.

She could see the conference room down the hall from where she sat. Seth was putting her destroyed clothes back into the evidence bags. Adrienne knew Conner would return soon.

Conner had agreed to drive her back to Lodi this afternoon so she could check on Vince and the horses. Adrienne knew it would do her good to get out of the city and away from the FBI for a little bit. They had planned to stay the night and come back tomorrow morning. But now Adrienne had a new plan, and she didn't think Conner was going to like it at all.

Adrienne looked down at the files on the desk and opened one in particular—the one she had worked on with the artist to try to pinpoint the location of where Simon Says was taking and killing the women. She knew she was missing something about this place. Something important. But she could never seem to find time to focus on it. Here at the FBI field office, or really anywhere in the city, there was too much outside interference. The only time she had quiet was when Conner was around.

She was so incredibly grateful for Conner. He had made this all bearable. Not just because of how he negated her abilities and gave her blessed silence. Adrienne had come to depend on him in other ways as well, and couldn't wait to go home with him each night.

Adrienne looked up just in time to see him walk into the conference room where Seth was still working. From the door he paused and turned in her direction. Seeing her watching him, he smiled and winked at her. Then turned and walked the rest of the way into the conference room.

Adrienne could feel her heart puddle at her feet. There was no doubt she was falling in love with that man. Everything about him fit her perfectly.

Adrienne giggled to herself, thinking about last night. Yes, *everything* about him fit her perfectly.

Closing the file and attempting to get her wayward

thoughts in check, Adrienne walked to the conference room. She knew what she needed to do. But she also knew Conner was not going to like it. Seth and Conner looked up from repacking the evidence bags as she entered.

"I've been thinking about Lodi," Adrienne stated from the doorway.

"Do you still want to go?" Conner asked.

"Yes. I need to. But, Conner, I don't think you should come with me."

Conner stopped the work he was doing and looked directly at her. "What?"

Adrienne held up the file in her hand. "I've been thinking about the place where Simon Says is killing the women. I feel like there's more about this that I can figure out."

"Okay. That would be great."

"But I can't do it with you around."

Conner shrugged. "Fine. Then do it here, and I'll leave again for a while."

Adrienne walked over to Conner and put her hand on his arm. "No. I don't want you to have to leave again. This is *your* office."

Conner began to protest, but Adrienne cut him off. "Besides, it's too mentally loud in this building. There are so many things trying to pull me away from focusing. And not just here in the building—in this entire city. I need some quiet. I want to take some of the photos with me to Lodi."

"And you can't do your magic if I'm there."

Adrienne ran her fingers down his arm and grasped his hand. "Yes. I'm sorry. But I know I'm missing something with these. Being alone where it's quiet might give me more insight."

"Alone? No way. Simon knows who you are. There's no reason to think he doesn't know where you live."

"Conner, I'll be able to know if Simon is around. He can't sneak up on me."

"That's fine. But if he somehow did get close to you, you would be totally helpless. I've seen what happens to you when you're just around things he's touched. What would you be like around him in person?" His expression hardened, determination glittering in his eyes. "There is no way in hell you're going by yourself."

"I'll take her," Seth chirped in. "We'll leave this afternoon and come back in the morning, just like you planned to do."

Adrienne could tell Conner didn't like it. Adrienne didn't much like the thought of being away from him, either. But there wasn't much way around it.

"I won't let her out of my sight, Scout's honor." Seth held up two fingers in some sort of incorrect scout salute. "I'll even sleep in the bed with her if she'll let me."

Conner rolled his eyes and put his arm around Adrienne. "Don't push it, Harrington." But Conner nodded. "I guess I should get caught up on some of the three hundred pounds of paperwork I have here."

Adrienne cringed. He hadn't been able to do any of his normal work in the past few days so that she could work here in safety.

"I'm sorry." Adrienne looked up at Conner. "I've pretty much kicked you out of your own office."

Conner kissed her quickly on the lips. "I would give up my office anytime if it meant you were safe. Plus, I like that at the Starbucks they know my order now as soon as I walk in. I am no longer mocked by the masses when ordering my drink of choice."

Seth smirked. "Happy for you, princess. You ready to go, Adrienne?"

"Sure. My stuff is by Conner's desk." She didn't have much since all of her clothes had been destroyed by Simon three days ago.

"Okay, I'll grab it and meet you at my car."

Conner walked with Adrienne out to the parking garage. "Stay with Seth the entire time. Don't even go to the barn without him. And definitely no riding."

Adrienne smiled. "I promise."

"I don't like you not being with me. I trust Seth with my life, but I wish I could be with you." He gently grabbed both sides of the collar of her shirt and pulled her up on her tiptoes. "I'll see you tomorrow."

Adrienne kissed him. "Yes, you will. And hopefully with more answers than I have right now."

Conner kissed her again. "I don't care about answers as much as I care about you getting back to me."

Adrienne could feel heat flood her center. "Me either," she said with a smile.

THE DRIVE TO the ranch was uneventful. Adrienne was relieved to see Vince and the horses—all in excellent shape. Vince truly was able to handle everything without her and even seemed a little disappointed to see her back. He immediately cheered when he found she would only be staying for the night.

Adrienne walked with Vince out to the barn. "You sure you've been doing okay?"

"Never better, Missy. You know I like it best when it's just me and the horses. No offense. Real question is, are *you* okay?"

Adrienne nodded. "It hasn't been as bad as I thought it might be, Vince. As a matter of fact, some of it has been downright nice. Maybe FBI agents aren't as bad as you and I made them out to be."

Vince grimaced. "I don't know about that. But I'm glad they're looking out for you."

"They're looking out for you, too, Vince. I don't think anyone is going to be bothering you about a missed parole anytime soon."

The older man looked decidedly relieved. Adrienne reached over and hugged him. He hugged her back in his stiff way. Adrienne left him alone in the barn and went back to the house.

Seth was a very active guard. All evening, he constantly checked windows and walked around the house. Perhaps that was because Conner called every hour for an update. Finally at 10:00 p.m. Conner switched to texts so he wouldn't disturb anyone else, but he evidently had no qualms about disturbing Seth. Adrienne wasn't worried about Simon Says at all.

Adrienne was glad to have the relative quiet of the ranch. She could hear the slight buzz of Vince and Seth, but that was easily ignored. It gave her the chance to study the pictures she had brought with her.

The pain was a constant as she looked at them, but she forced it aside. Although she had seen these images before—both the photos and the disjointed flashes of insight in her mind—they were still jarring. She focused on the building, the location where Simon Says was taking the women, and let everything else slide out of her mind.

Why couldn't she see the outside of the building? Always before she had been able to see a suspect entering or leaving their dwelling; that was one of the reasons she had been so helpful to the FBI—her ability to pinpoint location. *Bloodhound.*

But not now. Why?

It was too fuzzy for her. She could feel Simon's presence outside the building but couldn't see anything clearly. Just like when she had been touching her own clothes that Simon had destroyed.

Adrienne released the pictures and thought about that for a second. She had determined that Simon had been calm and methodical when he had destroyed her hotel room, not in any sort of vicious rage. So maybe Simon was calm and methodical when he brought the women to this place. Maybe he didn't have any desire to hurt them.

But that didn't make any sense. Why would he bring them there if he didn't have a desire to hurt them?

Then a thought occurred to Adrienne: was it possible Simon had a partner? Someone helping him bring the women into the building, but who had no desire to hurt them? Someone so meek and unassuming that Simon's personality all but overwhelmed the artifacts and pictures Adrienne had touched so she never felt the second person at all?

Adrienne went back through every picture again, one by one, searching for the presence of a second person, however minute. She could sense something different sometimes, but not always, and Simon's presence overshadowed whatever the lesser presence was.

Frustrated, Adrienne gave up on that line of thought. There was nothing in any of the evidence that had ever suggested Simon Says had a partner. He was too egotistical to share his control with someone else. Too sure of his own importance to leave details to someone else.

Exhausted, Adrienne decided to take a break. Simon having a partner was out of the question.

Adrienne wandered into the kitchen and found Seth making a pot of coffee.

"Planning to be up all night?"

Seth rubbed his face wearily. "Yeah. Someone's overprotective boyfriend keeps texting me every hour."

Adrienne winced. "Sorry."

"Don't worry about it. He was a pain in my butt long before you were around. Any luck with the pictures?"

Adrienne explained her theory about Simon having a possible partner, then all the reasons she had discarded it.

"It's worth keeping in consideration. Anything on location?"

"Nothing yet. I'm going to give it one more try in my room before I go to bed." Adrienne smiled at him. "I hope you get some sleep tonight."

She heard Seth mutter something under his breath but decided it was probably better not to ask him to repeat it.

In her bedroom, Adrienne changed into her pajamas and spread the pictures out on her bed. Once again she looked through each picture individually. It was all the same images as before. Nothing. Adrienne decided to look through them one last time and then give it a break. Maybe tomorrow would bring more clarity.

Even concentrating as hard as she was, she almost missed it.

She was studying the pictures of Josie Paton, the woman who had made Simon so angry because she refused to be scared. At first he had wanted to kill her quickly so he wouldn't have to hear her anymore. But he knew that would take all the pleasure out of it, so he decided to wait.

To calm himself down, he went for a walk. For just a

split second, as he went outside, she could see it. Some sort of old white mission-style church. Then Simon was having some sort of problem with vertigo, and it was all gone.

Adrienne went through the pictures with Josie Paton again just to be sure, but there was nothing else. But Simon having vertigo and a white church? Maybe those could be helpful. She would definitely tell Seth first thing in the morning. Right now she just wanted to get some sleep.

But lying in bed a few minutes later, Adrienne found sleep wouldn't come. She missed Conner. She'd only been without him for one night, but it felt like much longer. What was she going to do without him after they caught Simon? Adrienne didn't want to think about it. She closed her eyes and pushed the thought away.

Chapter Thirteen

Adrienne went from fast asleep to completely awake in an instant. She sat up in bed immediately alert. Had she heard something? What had woken her? Something definitely didn't seem right, but she couldn't figure out what it was.

Adrienne looked around, then stilled herself to listen. Nothing. It was still dark outside. She glanced at the clock—3:45 a.m.

Dressed in her pajama pants and T-shirt, she slipped out of her bedroom. Was Seth still in the living room or had he gone to sleep? Adrienne didn't know. She quietly made her way past the bathroom and down the hall. There was no need to wake anyone else up if there was nothing wrong.

But something felt wrong. Sort of. Nothing was hurting in her head, nor was she seeing any visions. But there was almost a residual evil presence. Like what Adrienne had been thinking about last night when she'd considered Simon Says might have a partner.

Adrienne entered the living room and saw Seth wasn't there. She had thought he might still be awake, but maybe Conner had finally given Seth some peace and quit texting, allowing Seth to sleep. Adrienne headed to the house's third bedroom, which had been converted into an office. Although the desk took up most of the space in the room, there was also a couch. Adrienne had left a pillow and blanket there for Seth in case he wanted them.

The door was cracked, so Adrienne peeked in. There on the couch lay the pillow and the blankets, still neatly folded. Seth had definitely not been here.

"Seth?" Adrienne called out. Something wasn't right. Adrienne no longer cared if she woke anybody else up. She rushed from the back bedroom to the kitchen, but found Seth wasn't there, either.

"Seth?" Adrienne called louder.

"What's going on?" Vince came out of his bedroom already dressed in his shirt and jeans but still looking sleepy.

"I'm looking for Seth. Agent Harrington. He wasn't in the living room or the office."

Adrienne didn't want to panic, but she didn't think Seth would've left her here without telling her.

"Maybe he ran out to his car to grab something."

That would make sense. But Adrienne hesitated to open the door and look. Instead she grabbed her cell phone from the table.

She called Conner.

"Are you okay?" he answered without greeting.

"I'm fine. Have you talked to Seth recently?"

"What time is it?" Adrienne could hear the sleepiness in Conner's voice.

"Almost four o'clock."

"I haven't talked to him in a couple of hours. Where is he?"

Adrienne was really getting frightened now. "I don't know, Conner. He was on the couch when I went to bed a few hours ago, but now he's not here. Seth wouldn't just *leave*."

Adrienne looked over at Vince, who was watching with concern. He shrugged.

Out of the corner of her eye she saw it then—in the window that faced the barn. Some weird orange glow in the darkness just past the house.

Adrienne walked over to the window to get a closer look. A chill overtook her as she realized what the orange glow was.

The barn was on fire!

Vince realized it at the same time and ran out the door as fast as he could with his limp. Almost forgetting about the phone in her hand, Adrienne was right behind him.

"Adrienne! What the hell is going on?"

"The barn is on fire, Conner!" Adrienne yelled to him as she ran.

"Adrienne, listen to me, you need to stay in the house. If Seth is gone, this could be Simon Says."

"I can't, Conner! I have to help Vince get the horses out!"

She could hear them now, their high-pitched screaming. Bucking as they tried to get out of their stalls and away from the fire that terrified them.

"Adrienne!" Conner roared from the phone. Adrienne stopped running at the urgency in his tone.

"Conner, I cannot do nothing while the horses are trapped. I just can't!"

"I know, baby. But listen to me. Do you have any weapons in the house? A handgun?"

"No, only a rifle."

"That's too big. Do you have any pepper spray or anything like that?"

"Yes."

"Get it and keep it with you. Or grab a kitchen knife if you have to. But be aware, Adrienne. Help Vince, but be mindful that Simon may be out there somewhere. I'll get locals on their way to you."

Adrienne couldn't hear anything else over the horses, so she ended the call. She spun and started running back toward the house. Conner was right. Although she couldn't feel him now, Simon could easily be out there somewhere, waiting for her. She had to help the horses, but she also had to protect herself.

In the kitchen, Adrienne grabbed the can of pepper spray in a drawer. She decided not to bring a knife; she would probably only cut herself. She headed in a dead sprint out to the barn.

The fire was quickly spreading, and the horses were becoming more panicked. Adrienne tried to remember what Conner said about Simon Says and awareness, but it was hard in all the chaos. She had to get the horses to safety.

Vince was making his way back out to the main barn door, dragging something. At first it looked to Adrienne like a huge bag of feed. She felt nausea pit in her stomach when she realized it was a person Vince was trying to drag out.

Seth.

Adrienne rushed over to help Vince.

"The FBI agent," Vince yelled. Adrienne grabbed one of Seth's arms, shuddering as she looked at the blood from an obvious head wound dripping down his face.

"Is he dead, Vince?" Adrienne couldn't bear the thought.

"No. Still breathing. We've got to get him away from here, then get in to help the horses."

They dragged Seth far enough away to be in no danger from the fire. He was still unconscious. Vince immediately returned to the barn, but Adrienne hesitated. She hated leaving Seth there alone, unprotected, but the horses were working their way into a complete frenzy. She had to go help Vince or all of them would die.

Adrienne turned back to the barn. The flames were climbing higher. From over to her right, she could see the flashing lights of emergency vehicles making their way, but they were still off in the distance. They wouldn't get there in time to help the horses. Only she and Vince could do that.

Adrienne dashed the rest of the way to the barn, the smoke getting thicker with every step she took. When she entered, she found she couldn't see anything because of the smoke. The horses, screaming and bucking in their terror, desperate to get out of the barn, made hearing impossible, too. She grabbed a nearby towel, dipped it in water from a bucket by the door and wrapped it around her head. She began looking for Vince but couldn't find him anywhere.

Unable to locate Vince, Adrienne decided to follow the sound of the horses. The first panicked one she found was Willie Nelson. Adrienne opened his stall and slowly walked toward the frightened animal, grabbing the halter and lead rope from the wall.

Although generally gentle by nature, Willie Nelson was beyond reason now. He nipped at Adrienne and kicked at the barn walls with his hind legs. Adrienne knew if she couldn't get the halter on him in the next few seconds, she would have to leave him behind and go for another horse. Seconds were precious.

From out of nowhere a hand grabbed Adrienne's shoulder. Terror shot through her. She reached for the pepper spray, but it was deep in her pocket and she couldn't quite get it out. She let out a high-pitched scream as the hand roughly spun her around.

It was Vince.

Adrienne almost sagged in relief, seeing the older man. He didn't seem to notice any of her strange behavior.

"The only way to get them out of the barn is to blindfold them and then put on the halter," he yelled over the horses' screams and the sound of the fire. He threw a few short towels at Adrienne and ran back out of the stall.

Adrienne approached Willie Nelson again, towel in hand. After a couple of tries, Adrienne was able to get the towel over his head. Unable to see, he immediately calmed. Adrienne quickly led him from the barn and into a nearby fenced corral, far enough from the fire to keep the horses from panicking. Two other horses were already there.

That meant there were five more left in the barn.

Adrienne sprinted back, coughing as she entered the barn's barrage of black smoke again. Everything hurt: her lungs, her throat, her head, her eyes—but she knew she couldn't stop.

Adrienne found another horse and followed the same procedure as she had with Willie Nelson. It was getting harder to breathe, and the heat was now beginning to truly become a factor. Adrienne knew she wouldn't be able to make many more trips before the fire would overwhelm the barn completely.

As she made it to the barn door, she looked up, shocked to see Seth stumbling unsteadily toward her.

"Give me the horse. I can get it to the corral."

Adrienne coughed and looked at the blood dripping down his face. "Are you sure?"

Seth didn't try to answer, just took the lead from Adrienne and slowly began walking the horse away from the barn. As Adrienne turned to go back inside she saw some movement on the front porch of the house. In the dark it was difficult to tell, but it looked like someone was sitting in one of the rocking chairs on her front porch.

Simon Says.

Adrienne knew it was him. Could feel the pounding in her head clearly now. Could feel his glee at the chaos he had caused.

Adrienne deliberately turned away and went back inside the barn. Let the bastard watch. She was going to get every single one of her horses out. She wouldn't let Simon win this sick little game. She didn't think he was going to harm her; it looked like he was more interested in watching from the sidelines.

But she made sure the pepper spray was easily reachable in her pocket just to be sure.

Five minutes later she and Vince had gotten all the horses out. Thanks to Seth's help, all the horses were safe, if very spooked, in the corral. When Adrienne looked up at the porch again, it was empty. And her head no longer hurt.

Simon was gone.

Not long afterward, the fire department arrived. Adrienne, Seth and Vince sat exhausted on the back steps of the house and watched as they put out the fire and saved what was left of the barn.

Adrienne was relieved that they were all safe and relatively unharmed. A paramedic had looked at Seth's head wound and announced he probably had a concussion and should go to the local hospital. Adrienne and Vince had been given oxygen and told they suffered from smoke inhalation and should also go.

But none of them did. Instead they sat on the back steps almost too exhausted to move. They would live.

The sun began to work its way up over the landscape. The rising sun somehow made everything seem a little better. The sound of a vehicle squealing into the driveway made things even better for Adrienne.

Conner was here. One hour and twenty-six minutes after she had called him. She would bet he had broken quite a few traffic laws to get here this quickly.

She watched as he walked toward the barn. She would've called out to him but knew her voice would never carry in the state it was in. She saw him notice where they sat. He turned midstride and quickly made his way over to them, eyes only on Adrienne.

Adrienne was too tired to even stand and hug him. Not that he would want her to hug him—she must look and smell like a chimney.

Conner sat down on the step right next to her. He reached over, picked her up and deposited her in his lap. His arms came around her in a crushing hug.

"Thank God."

Adrienne could barely breathe from the force of his hug but didn't care.

"I knew I should've never let you come to Lodi without me."

"Conner." Adrienne wiggled until she could get her arms out from under his and put them around him. "I'm okay. It's all okay."

She was here with him now, safe in his arms. Eventually he loosened his grasp to a more reasonable level.

He studied her face intently then reached down and touched her just over her lip.

"Simon was here."

Startled, Adrienne peeked up at him. "Yes, he was. How did you know?"

"Your nose was bleeding."

Out of habit Adrienne tried to wipe it with the back of her hand. She was sure that just got more soot on her face.

"I saw him, Conner. He was sitting on the other side of the house on the front porch. He was in a rocking chair watching us get the horses out."

"Could you see him well enough to make out any features?" Conner asked.

"No, it was too dark. I guess I could probably feel him there more than I could actually see him."

She couldn't make out features, but she knew she had seen someone in one of the rocking chairs.

"But he didn't try to hurt you?"

"No. Clocked Seth cold, though," Adrienne told him.

Conner looked over at Seth, who nodded his head gingerly. "Yeah, I thought I saw a light in the barn and I went to check it out. Stupid. Didn't find anything so was on my way back inside when he caught me on the steps. Dragged me back to the barn."

Adrienne sighed. "That must be what woke me up. I thought I heard something, but maybe I just felt Simon when he was that close to the house."

Seth grimaced. "Maybe. Whatever it was, I'm glad you woke up when you did. He definitely intended for me to die in that barn. If Vince hadn't gotten there when he did…"

Seth trailed off. Adrienne didn't blame him.

"Could you feel Simon Says while you were getting the horses out of the barn?" Conner asked.

"Yeah. But everything was loud and chaotic and painful, so I didn't let it stop me."

Two uniformed police officers walked around the side of the house. Conner set Adrienne down on the step beside him and stood up to talk to them. Seth joined them. She saw them both show the officers their FBI credentials.

Vince looked over at her. "Guess you and that FBI officer don't hate each other so much now."

Adrienne was not so exhausted that she couldn't flush. Hopefully the soot hid it. "Yeah. He ended up not being so bad after all."

Vince chuckled. It was the first time Adrienne remembered the sound coming from the older man. "I've decided to like him," Vince finally said.

Adrienne was shocked. She didn't think Vince would like an agent for any reason. "Oh, yeah? Why?"

"He just picked you up and plopped you down right on top of him—and no offense, girly, but you look and smell terrible—without any concern for his clothes whatsoever. That's a man who's got his priorities straight."

Adrienne smiled. She thought so, too.

After a few minutes of talking to the officers, Conner and Seth made their way back to the steps where Vince and Adrienne waited, still too tired to move. Both Seth and Conner looked grim. Conner had some sort of paper in his hand.

Conner sat back down next to Adrienne. "It was definitely Simon you saw on the porch."

Adrienne didn't have any doubt of that. "Did you find something?"

Conner held up an envelope. Adrienne immediately recognized it. She had seen ones just like it multiple times. Simon's literal calling card.

Conner opened it and read the note.

Simon says, thanks for the show!

So Adrienne had been right. He had been there, watching, reveling in their frantic attempts to save the livestock. Maybe his initial intent had been to harm Adrienne, but he had gotten caught up in watching their efforts in the chaos he had created.

Nobody said anything for a long while. It was finally Vince who broke the silence as he stood up. "I don't know who this 'Simon' character is, but I don't care for him much. He and I are going to have words if he ever sets foot on this property again. But right now I'm going to see if I can get some of this burnt barn smell off me, before it drives the womenfolk mad with desire."

Both men chuckled, and Adrienne grinned.

Conner bent his head and kissed her. "You did a good job, you know."

Adrienne slumped exhaustedly against his arm. "We all did. All the horses survived. We all survived. Simon didn't win this time."

But they knew Simon wouldn't stop trying until he had.

Chapter Fourteen

It took days before Adrienne was able to get back to San Francisco. She had to find temporary boarding situations for all the horses, complete an endless number of insurance forms and find contractors to begin rebuilding the barn. It was tedious work.

Conner stayed by her side the entire time.

Seth headed back to San Francisco the day after the fire, once he and Conner had finished processing the scene—what was left of it, anyway.

Simon Says had very definitely started the barn fire. He'd made no attempt to hide where his arson was initiated—in one of the far stalls where no horses were housed, thank God—or his use of accelerants to help the flames along.

All in all, the arson detective said it was a miracle no people or animals had been killed.

Having her own FBI agent able to explain the nature of the foul play to the insurance inspectors made the process much more streamlined. Adrienne was thankful to have Conner around every day. And every night.

Conner was always by her side. Always watchful in case Simon struck again. Somehow Simon had made it through Adrienne's mental warning system before, although Adrienne blamed it on sleep rather than on Simon being far away in the barn. But Conner was still very vigilant.

Four days after the fire, Adrienne was finally able to get the ranch and rebuilding of the barn to a state where she could leave. Vince was overseeing the construction, and the horses were all gone—there wasn't much at the ranch she was needed for. So she and Conner decided to return to the city.

Although he had never said anything outright, Adrienne could tell Conner was anxious to get back to the office where he could work. He wanted to protect her. She knew the best way he could do that was to catch Simon Says. Conner's very personality demanded he be more active in that pursuit, not reactive, waiting with her.

Adrienne knew as soon as they entered the ViCAP office areas later that morning that something had happened. She and Conner headed directly for Conner's and Seth's desks amid the buzz.

"What's going on?" Conner asked.

"Another package from Simon arrived a little bit ago," Seth said. "I was waiting for you guys to get here to open it."

Conner grimaced. "Okay, I'll get out of here."

"You're not going to stay and open it?" Adrienne touched Conner lightly on the arm.

"No. I might as well just let you do your thing from the get-go. Seth will catch anything I would see." Conner shifted away from Adrienne, not overtly rejecting her touch, but definitely not welcoming it. Adrienne understood his frustration but was still hurt.

"Conner, I'm sorry." Adrienne couldn't stand the distance between them, the tension.

"No, don't you apologize." Conner didn't move any closer to her, but his eyes warmed. "This is me—my problem. I have to learn to deal with it."

"I'm still sorry." Adrienne ached for him.

Now Conner did move closer to her. "You're too tenderhearted to do this." He ran a finger down her cheek. "I don't know how you've survived this long with all your emotions still functional."

Adrienne smiled, but the truth was, sometimes neither did she.

Conner stepped back, putting a more appropriate workplace distance between them. "I'll just be a few blocks down. Seth's going to stream it live to my phone again."

Seth called from the conference room. They were ready to open the package. Adrienne turned toward the room, but Conner caught her waist and jerked her back to him.

His lips fell heavily on hers, stealing her breath. Before she could say or do anything, he moved away, pushing her gently toward the conference room. "Go do your thing, sweetheart. Let's catch this guy." Conner grabbed his jacket.

Adrienne started walking but turned back. Being back in the office had reminded her. "After this, make sure I show you what I found before the fire. It's in the file. I might have some details about Simon's hideout, although right now they're pretty useless."

Conner smiled. "I'll look it over with you when I get back."

It made Adrienne feel better knowing Conner was watching from his phone. It wouldn't stop her physical discomfort, but emotionally it helped her gear up. It was good having Conner as close as possible.

Adrienne stood in the corner of the conference room as Seth opened the outer package. She could hear the buzzing getting louder, so she knew Conner was out of the building. One of the other agents—Adrienne vaguely remembered seeing him around—was holding the camera so Conner would be able to see what was going on.

It was the same as all the others. A lock of hair and a note.

Simon says, hurry.

Decidedly less mocking than the other notes Simon had sent. But yet, not helpful in any way. All the people in the room—mostly agents, but a couple photographers and even an analyst—looked disappointed at the content of the box. What were they expecting exactly? Adrienne had no idea.

Seth wasted no time shooing them out of the conference room so Adrienne wouldn't have an audience while she worked. After last time, that was important to her. The less noise and distractions around, the better.

"Ready?" Seth asked. Only he and the agent holding the camera remained. Adrienne nodded and took a deep breath.

Knowing that touching the lock of hair would show her the murder and wanting to put that off for as long as possible, Adrienne reached out for the note. The notes always told her more about Simon anyway. The hair was too enmeshed with the victim—her fears and feelings. The note was solely Simon.

Unlike before, this time Adrienne immediately could envision a place. A theater, complete with a stage and props and lighting.

All the world's a stage, And all the men and women

merely players. They have their exits and their en-
trances; and one man in his time plays many parts...

Simon standing on this stage quoting Shakespeare
to an invisible audience. So sure of his own importance
and intellect. Adrienne couldn't see his face but could
hear his voice.

His voice didn't match what he thought of himself
in his head. He believed himself to be powerful and
potent, but his voice was high and whiny, and would
never demand respect.

Adrienne wished she could tell him this to his face.
But she knew he'd kill her for it. An image—memory—
flashed through the killer's mind and Adrienne understood why he had picked the women he had.

Not because of their appearance or because they'd
all shopped or visited the same locations. He had picked
them because they reminded him of a woman from his
past, from his childhood. Simon just thought of the
woman as "her."

Adrienne didn't know exactly who *this woman* was
to Simon, but she had made him feel weak and power-
less. She had mocked and ridiculed him. Especially his
voice—so high-pitched, as if he had never become a
man. Would never become a man. A whiny little girl,
she had called him. He hated her. His hatred of her overshadowed everything about him.

It wasn't their looks that caused him to choose his
victims. It was their *voices*.

His memory of *her* was soon pushed away by Simon.
He took a bow before his invisible audience, then looked
up toward the spotlight and waved. He jumped down
from the stage and walked straight down the aisle out
the front entrance to the street outside.

Then, in an almost deliberate motion, he turned and looked up at the sign.

"The Eureka Theater." Adrienne said the name out loud. She let go of the letter and looked over at Seth. "Did you get that?"

"Yes. Eureka Theater. It's across town. We're calling locals now. Conner's on his way back."

"No. Tell him to wait a minute. Seth, there's something not right here."

"What?"

"I don't know. Let me touch the hair. Something's different."

Seth relayed the message to Conner over the phone. Adrienne could hear Conner's curses even from where she stood. But she knew she had to do this to figure out what was going on.

Taking a deep breath again, she reached her fingers out and touched just the tiniest part. She braced herself, prepared for the worst.

But she had not prepared herself for this. She reached down and clutched the entire lock of hair in her fist, to be sure.

Adrienne couldn't help herself, she began sobbing. Seth tried to talk to her, but she couldn't stop. Seth put his phone up to Adrienne's ear, so she could hear Conner.

"Adrienne, baby, I know it's hard. But I need you to tell us what you see."

"Conner…she's alive. She's still alive!"

Everything was a blur after that moment. Conner was back in the building within two minutes. He and Seth wanted to know every detail of what she had seen. Was Adrienne sure the woman was still alive? Yes. Was Adrienne sure she was at the Eureka Theater? Yes.

Was Adrienne sure this was a trap? Yes.

She couldn't seem to make them understand. Conner rushed past her to get to his desk and Adrienne followed. "Conner, there's something else. I can't quite figure it out. Everything about this screams 'trap.' You have to be careful."

Conner put his hands on either side of Adrienne's neck and rubbed her cheeks with his thumbs. "We will be careful. I promise."

Adrienne grasped his wrists. "I want to come with you."

She could feel him stiffen. "No. No way in hell. You just said this was a trap. You're not a trained agent. And after the fire— You being at the crime scene unprotected? No, that's just what he wants. Stay here where you're safe."

"I want to help."

"It helps me knowing you're here, safe."

"What if you need me? My abilities?"

Conner reached down and kissed her lightly. "We'll get someone to bring you if we need you. I promise. Just stay here and be safe."

He was out of her arms and running down the hall with Seth before she could even respond.

THIS WAS THE break they had been waiting for. The excitement was palpable in the area outside the Eureka Theater. The local police had been the first to arrive but had waited—as ordered—for the FBI. They had secured all entrances and exits, making sure no one had come in or out.

Conner had no idea why the girl was still alive— if the package had just arrived earlier than Simon expected or if something had gone wrong. Regardless he did not take Adrienne's warning lightly. If she suspected this may be a trap, they would treat it as such.

The bomb squad had pulled in just ahead of Seth and Conner, and were now inspecting the doors for explosives. Conner watched with barely restrained anxiety. Was there a woman in there suffering while they were taking so long out here? Could she possibly be bleeding out even now, and they would be too late to help her?

Could Simon still be inside the building?

They had to be cautious, Conner understood, but everything in him screamed to get inside that theater as soon as possible. The minutes it took for the bomb squad to determine the front door safe seemed like hours. Once the front door was opened, the bomb dogs were allowed inside to sniff out any explosives.

It wasn't long before they found something.

In a breakaway door, just under the stage, a grouping of explosives had been set. Some sort of remote detonation device was attached to it. The bomb squad was able to disarm and remove it without anyone being harmed.

Adrienne had been right—it had been a trap. If the local police or FBI had rushed into the theater without the bomb squad, many more lives would've been lost. Her gift had saved untold lives today.

After another thorough sweep of the building by the dogs, it was deemed safe—at least from explosives—to enter. Conner and Seth were the first inside, weapons drawn. Certainly bombs weren't the only danger Simon Says could've laid out for them.

They cautiously made their way through the theater, calling out for anyone who might be in there, but received no response. Conner and Seth, along with the other officers, began systematically checking through the aisles for anyone who might be on the ground, out of sight. They checked the stage with even more caution but found nothing. Discouragement began to sink in. Perhaps the woman wasn't really here at all.

Conner stood on the stage looking out where law enforcement of all different types were searching through all the seats of the theater for anything—or anybody—who may be hidden there. There were others behind him, searching through the stage and the backstage area, but so far had come up empty.

Seth came over to Conner. "Think this is a bust?"

"I don't want to think so, but…" Conner shrugged. The frustration in both of them was close to boiling over. And standing in the damn spotlights aimed at the stage was causing them to sweat.

"'All the world's a stage…'" Conner said it out loud, remembering watching from his phone as the words had come out of Adrienne's mouth an hour ago. Not her words, but Simon's. Well, actually Shakespeare's, from *As You Like It,* if Conner remembered his college literature class correctly.

"Yeah, Simon obviously thinks of himself as the playwright in this ridiculous scene." Seth grimaced.

Conner went over everything Adrienne had said in his head. Then looked up at the spotlight. Although all the house lights had been turned on when they had entered the building, none of the other stage lights were burning. Why were these?

"Seth, Adrienne said Simon looked up at the spotlight and waved, right before he jumped off the stage and ran down the aisle to the front door. He had to have been standing right here when he did that."

"Damn, Con. Why is that light even on? It wouldn't have been on the house lights switch."

They both sprinted to the metal ladder leading up

to the theater's catwalk. They quickly made their way to where the spotlight stood attached to a lighting batten. Sure enough, there lay a young woman, bound and gagged.

But very much alive.

"We found her! We need a medic up here," Seth yelled out, as Conner reached down to remove the gag wrapped around the woman's head. She immediately began sobbing.

"Are you all right?" Conner asked her, helping her sit up. "Are you injured in any way?"

The woman shook her head. "No, I'm f-fine…" The medic rushed over the catwalk to where Conner knelt beside the woman. Conner stood to give him room. He wanted to ask the woman questions, but it could wait the few minutes until she was checked out. Conner watched as the medic cut away the zip-tie that tied her hands and feet, and checked over her body for broken bones or injury. When he got to her back, the medic stopped. Frowning, he unpinned something that was attached to the woman's clothing.

"Special Agent Perigo?" The medic looked over at Conner.

"Yes?" Conner frowned at Seth then looked over at the medic. How did the medic know his name?

"I think this is for you." He handed Conner a note with his name on the front. Seth rushed over as Conner opened it.

Simon says, never mind. I found someone better.

WAITING AT CONNER'S desk back at the field office, Adrienne thought she might go out of her mind. They hadn't heard anything from the crime scene—that was good news. If anything catastrophic had happened, they would've heard about it.

That still didn't stop her from worrying. Had they found the woman? Was she alive? Had Simon Says tried anything to hurt them?

Adrienne ran her hands over her face wearily. Being here in this office was painful without Conner. Too much buzzing, too many voices and images trying to push their way through to her mind. She had to constantly battle to keep them out. It was exhausting.

Adrienne looked down at the file she had brought in with her—the picture of Josie Paton still on top. Maybe she could start searching for this church she had seen. But there were hundreds of churches in San Francisco. Adrienne had no idea where to begin.

Or maybe she should focus on Simon's vertigo. Was that something requiring medical treatment? Could the FBI find a record of him through that? And why had Simon seemed so happy about his vertigo?

Adrienne did a quick search of vertigo on the computer to get an understanding of exactly what it was. *A feeling of motion when one is stationary.* It seemed like a dead end, not something likely to require long-term medical treatment or records.

Adrienne spotted it as she was about to turn the computer off.

Vertigo. Vertigo with a capital *V.* The famous Alfred Hitchcock movie.

As soon as she read it, everything clicked into place. Simon didn't have vertigo. He was thinking of the famous scene from *Vertigo* while he stood outside San Francisco's Mission Dolores Basilica. Simon was proud he was right in the middle of the most upper crust of San

Francisco, and no one was any the wiser. That was why he was so gleeful when he thought of the word *vertigo*.

Adrienne printed out a map of Dolores Street and the surrounding areas. Based on Simon's thoughts about the church, and the inside of the building she had seen, there were only a few places where his hideout could be. Adrienne marked them carefully on the map. As soon as Conner and Seth got back, she would take them there.

She briefly considered going there herself, but deemed it too stupid to act on. Wasn't that always how people got killed in movies—by doing something brash and alone like that? But she definitely wanted to take Conner and Seth to check it out as soon as they could.

"Ms. Jeffries?" One of the FBI photographers rushed up to where she sat at Conner's desk. What was his name? Adrienne had seen him around but couldn't remember.

"Yes? I'm sorry I've forgotten your name."

The man smiled, but Adrienne could tell the smile didn't reach his eyes. "I'm Victor Faraday, a photographer. A report just came in from the scene everyone is at."

Adrienne stood up. "Yes?"

"Evidently there was a woman dead by the time they got there."

Adrienne was crushed. She was so sure the woman had been alive. Maybe they had been too late.

"There's no cell phone coverage in the theater, so Special Agent Perigo couldn't call you. But he had someone radio in and wants you out there as soon as possible."

Adrienne took a deep breath. Another crime scene. She wasn't looking forward to it. "Sure, I'm ready whenever."

"Okay, I'll give you a ride, if you want. I've got to go out there, too."

Adrienne hesitated for just a second. She had seen Victor around, but she didn't really know him. But she knew if he had any malicious intent toward her she would sense it, since Conner wasn't around. "That would be great, Victor. Thanks so much."

They walked together down to the parking lot and got into Victor's SUV. Adrienne was overwhelmed again with sadness that the woman was dead. The last time Simon Says had seen her, she had been alive, that much Adrienne knew from touching the lock of hair he had sent. Something must have happened to her between the time Simon had left and when the FBI had gotten to the theater.

Adrienne didn't know where the theater was, so she was glad Victor was driving. As they got farther away from the FBI building Adrienne noticed the visions and voices pressing in on her were getting more insistent rather than less. Usually outside the FBI office, the noise got a little softer—there weren't so many suspects and so much evidence trying to tell its story to her.

But something in this vehicle was demanding her attention. She looked over at Victor—it wasn't him. She looked around and noticed how dark all the windows were tinted.

"Your windows are really dark."

Victor nodded at her. "Yes, I had to get a special permit for the tinting. It keeps sun off my equipment. Also helps prevent theft."

Maybe that was it. Theft. Maybe someone had tried to break into this SUV recently, and that was what Adrienne was picking up on. Whatever it was, it was getting worse.

Adrienne rubbed her head. She reached into her purse for some aspirin.

"Head hurt?" Victor asked.

"Yeah. I'm not sure what's going on."

"I hope it feels better soon."

Adrienne looked over at Victor sharply. Was she imagining things or did his voice just change a little bit? Become a little higher. And a little more whiny.

Just like the voice she had heard in her head earlier when she had opened Simon's note.

The SUV pulled up to a curb and stopped. But they weren't at the Eureka Theater. They were in front of the building Adrienne had been scoping out and researching this morning. The building where Simon was killing his victims.

Adrienne turned to Victor to get a good look at him and watched as everything about his demeanor changed before her eyes. He went from an unassuming, soft-spoken photographer to a furious, violent killer Adrienne had never seen.

Without warning everything in Adrienne's head exploded as the malice radiating from Victor hit her. She felt her nose begin bleeding, and she barely held on to consciousness under the onslaught.

"Victor?"

A high-pitched voice—not Victor's—responded in a whiny tone. "Sorry, Victor's not here right now. I'm Simon. And I'm going to need a little piece of your hair."

Chapter Fifteen

Conner and Seth arrived back at the FBI field office a few hours later, happy they had gotten to the woman and the trap had been avoided. This entire situation definitely had been a departure from Simon's usual course of action. What Conner couldn't figure out was the why of it all. If it wasn't for Adrienne's description and explanation of the scene and the note found with the woman, Conner wouldn't have believed it was Simon at all.

After answering what questions she could—and there weren't very many she could answer since she had not seen or heard much of anything that could give them a lead on Simon—the woman had been taken to the hospital. She was dehydrated and scared out of her mind, but otherwise unharmed. Conner planned to take Adrienne to see her as soon as possible, and take Adrienne to the Eureka Theater, to see if she could pick up anything.

He had been trying to call Adrienne since they had found the woman alive. He knew Adrienne would want to know, that it would perhaps lift some of the burden she carried. But Adrienne wasn't picking up her cell. Conner knew the field office was a difficult and mentally loud place for her to be without him, so he wasn't surprised she wasn't paying attention to her phone. He was excited to be able to tell her face-to-face.

Conner was also anxious for Adrienne to provide her insight on what the newest note meant. *Simon says, never mind. I found someone better.* Upon reading that note, Conner's first thought had been concern for Adrienne. But he had believed Adrienne when she had said she would see Simon coming—he couldn't sneak up on her. In order for Simon to take her, he would have to use brute force, which wasn't going to happen with Adrienne in the middle of an FBI office.

Conner tried Adrienne's cell again as he walked into the office from the garage. Things should be quieter in her head now he was back. But there was still no answer.

"Dammit," Conner muttered.

"Still can't get a hold of Adrienne?"

"No. I can understand why she didn't answer while we were at the crime scene. But I thought she'd answer now."

There was more urgency to both their steps as they headed from the elevator down the hall to their desks. Conner scanned the area for Adrienne but didn't see her. Maybe she was in the conference room. The office seemed to be buzzing with activity. Conner understood why a moment later when Victor Faraday came up to him with a package in his hands.

"Agent Perigo?" Faraday said. "This came in a few minutes ago. I was already coming through the security area, so they asked me to bring it to you."

Conner frowned. Another package had arrived from Simon Says? He and Seth looked at each other without saying anything. Two packages in one day? Something was definitely not right.

"Has it already been scanned and vetted?" Seth asked.

Faraday nodded enthusiastically. "Yes, sir. It was cleared to bring up here. This one was different. It was left by the door, not mailed."

"Thanks." Conner took the package from Faraday. Faraday nodded again and gave Conner a weird smile. The man was acting odd, but, hell, they all acted odd every time a package came in.

Chief Kelly met them at their desks. "That the new package?"

"Yeah, we just got it," Seth responded. "We haven't opened it. This one is different—it wasn't mailed."

"Has it been scanned?" the chief asked. After the close call with the explosives earlier today, they weren't going to take any chances.

"Yes, came through clean," Conner told him. He looked for Faraday to reconfirm, but the photographer was gone.

Chief Kelly looked down at the package. "Okay, let's not waste any time. Get Adrienne and let's open it."

Conner felt something in his gut tighten. "Adrienne's not already in the conference room?"

"No. She was here earlier, waiting for you guys. You haven't seen her since you got back?"

Conner already had his phone out of his pocket and was dialing her number again. It went straight to voice mail.

"Con, don't panic," Seth told him. "She didn't know how long we were going to be gone. Maybe she's down at the coffee shop or out at one of the parks. You know how this building can become too much for her."

Conner took a deep breath. What Seth said made sense. But something was not sitting right with Conner.

"Perigo, we need to get this package opened," Chief Kelly told him. "If Simon Says is changing his pattern, this may be our best opportunity to catch him. Adrienne will show up soon."

Conner nodded, and they walked into the conference room where the new package sat. After donning gloves, they opened the outer box. It once again held a jewelry case, like always, and light enough only to hold a lock of hair. They opened it and found a lock—but instead of blond, as it had always been, the lock of hair was brown.

Brown with reddish tones. Conner knew the hair perfectly. He looked over at Seth who seemed to have lost all color. Conner took the note from Seth's nerveless fingers.

Simon says, it's not so easy without your little cheater, is it?

It took a moment for the facts to truly sink in. However impossible it seemed, Simon had Adrienne.

Conner heard shocked responses from around the room but couldn't quite make out what they were saying. The panic seized Conner in such a way that he could barely function. That psycho had Adrienne.

Was she already dead?

Conner pushed that thought completely from his mind. There was no way he would be able to function if he even allowed that thought to enter his head. Adrienne was not dead.

"Perigo!" Conner finally heard the chief who had evidently called his name more than once.

"Chief?"

"Keep it together, Perigo. We're going to find her."

Conner tamped down the panic deep inside. Chief Kelly was right. He had to keep it together if he wanted to be any help to Adrienne at all. He turned away from the package.

Thinking about what had happened today, Conner could see it was a perfect setup. Simon had gotten them away from Adrienne with the only possible thing that assured they would leave—live bait. Adrienne had sensed it was a trap from the beginning—and it had been, just for her, not for them.

Simon had even planted those explosives at the scene to draw them off the scent of his real plan. And it had worked beautifully. Caught up in all the prospective danger at the crime scene, Conner had hardly been worried about Adrienne at all.

Conner turned to Seth. "The woman we rescued this morning was never one of Simon's intended victims. Adrienne had always been the next target. We played right into his hands."

"Chief," Seth asked. "Did you see Adrienne here while we were gone?"

"Yeah. I saw her. She was talking to that photographer Victor Faraday when I saw her last."

"I'll go find him and see if he saw anything," Seth offered.

"I'm going to see if I can track her phone. Worked before." Conner headed to his desk to access the Bureau's network. Not long after putting in her phone's information, it came up with a location.

A spark of hope grew in Conner's chest until he saw the address. Her phone was somewhere inside the FBI field office.

Conner slammed his fist down on his desk. A few moments later Seth came rushing up.

"Faraday's gone, Conner. I went out and checked the garage myself and found this." Seth held out a phone. Conner slid the power button to On and saw the last seven missed calls were from him. This was definitely Adrienne's phone.

Chief Kelly walked up to their desks. The way he sighed, Conner knew the news was not good. "We pulled the camera footage from the parking garage camera. She definitely left with Faraday earlier today, about two hours before you guys got back."

The confusion that coursed through Conner quickly gave way to rage. Victor Faraday was Simon Says? How was that even possible? They had worked with the man for years.

And that bastard had been right here next to him, just a few minutes ago. Had the nerve to hand Conner a package, and *smile* at him, after he had already taken Adrienne.

The murderous rage was almost as incapacitating as the gut-wrenching fear Conner had felt when they had opened Simon's package. It also had to be pushed away so Conner could function.

"I've already checked with security. No second package came in today. Faraday must have brought it in himself and said it was found outside the door," the chief told them.

"We need every bit of information we have on Faraday. Right now." Conner announced, eyes hardening.

It turned out every bit of information they had on Victor Faraday was not a great deal. He had worked for the San Francisco field office for two years, having transferred from the Austin, Texas, field office. A search through the Bureau's systems confirmed a rash of unsolved murders had occurred in the Austin area around the same time Faraday had lived there. Once he had transferred here, the murders there had stopped.

"Hell if I can remember anything specific about him at all," Seth said with disgust, throwing Faraday's file on his desk. "Two years of working with him and I could barely pick him out of a lineup."

"He's played us from the start." Conner sighed roughly. "It's part of the reason Simon was always a step ahead of us."

"How do you think he got around Adrienne's abilities?" Seth asked.

"That's what I can't figure out. She should've been able to sense him coming. Hell, she should've sensed him the first time she was in the building. Or at least whenever I wasn't around. I don't understand it. She never had any specific insight to Simon at all. Except…"

Conner couldn't believe he had forgotten it. This morning Adrienne had come in all excited about a possible location where Simon—Faraday—might be keeping the women before he killed them. In the excitement of a new package and a live victim, her discovery had been pushed aside.

But she had given him a file, put it on his desk. Conner quickly tore through the papers on his desk. He found it and pulled out the map and information she had written. Mission Delores Basilica. She had highlighted the few places she thought could be Simon's hideout.

Conner was almost giddy with relief.

"Seth, I forgot until now. This is a map Adrienne left me. She mentioned something this morning. It's where she thought Simon Says was taking and killing the women."

Both men stood. It wasn't much, but it was better

than sitting here looking at files on Victor Faraday. Within moments, both men were sprinting for the car.

ADRIENNE WOKE UP to the screaming in her head. The noise and pain made her thoughts work slowly. She couldn't figure out where she was or how she had gotten there. She took deep breaths, trying to calm herself and focus.

She realized she was lying on the ground and her arms were restrained in front of her. The floor was hard, uncarpeted. She turned her body as gently as she could, so she could look around the room. High ceilings with dark rafters. A stairway that led to a thick door. No windows. It was an oversize cellar.

Through the fog of her brain Adrienne realized she had seen this place before. In her visions about Simon Says. It all came back to her then. Victor Faraday had brought her here. Victor Faraday was Simon Says.

"There you are. I thought you were never going to wake up. I tied you up while I was gone, but it looks like I don't really need to, do I?" A high-pitched giggle caused Adrienne to cringe in pain. Her fog-permeated brain could not figure out where the voice was coming from.

She knew she had to keep Simon talking. She could feel his malice—the terrible things he planned to do to her.

He had no plans for her to be alive in the next hour.

The agony of remaining conscious was almost more than Adrienne could bear. But she forced herself to focus. She could see Simon now. He was sitting on a wooden crate just a few feet from her.

"Where did you go?"

"Had to drop off the package to the FBI, of course.

I couldn't mail it. That would take too long. I wanted them to know I had you today. Right now." That high-pitched giggle again. Adrienne was sure her head would explode. "Victor just waltzed right in and handed it to your boyfriend."

So Conner had made it back from the other crime scene. That was good. He would figure it out and come for her, Adrienne knew that. They were at the place Adrienne had noted down and left for Conner in the file.

But would he remember it in the midst of everything going on? Would he get here in time?

Adrienne had to give Conner as much time as she could. She had to keep Simon talking.

"So Victor just walked in?"

"Yep. They didn't suspect a thing. I was sad he couldn't stick around and see Agent Perigo's face when he read the letter." Simon walked around her as she lay on the floor. Adrienne flinched away from him no matter where he was. She didn't want him to touch her, even by accident.

"You know," Simon said in his grating, singsongy voice, "I'm not surprised you and Conner fell in love with one another. It was fate."

Just keep him talking. "Oh, yeah. Why is that?"

"I like to look up what people's names mean. *Simon* means 'to be heard.' Don't you think that's perfect for me? I have always known I was meant to be heard." The giggle again. "Do you know what *Conner* means?"

Adrienne didn't want to talk about Conner with this sick bastard. "What?" she muttered through teeth grit-ted in pain and annoyance.

"*Conner* means lover of hounds." Simon clapped his hands like an enthusiastic second grader. "Don't you get it? *Conner* means lover of *hounds*. Like *bloodhounds*.

And you are known as 'the Bloodhound.' So apropos! Just perfect in every way."

Adrienne smiled just a bit through the pain. Conner probably wouldn't like knowing that's what his name meant. Too much like getting her name and picture tattooed on his skin.

But, "lover of hounds"? Somehow the nickname she had hated so much all those years ago didn't seem so terrible anymore. Not if it linked her with Conner.

Adrienne knew she was getting loopy. She needed to concentrate.

But it was so hard to think clearly with Simon so close. The pain was overwhelming.

"But not all names are correct," Simon continued as sadly now as he was delighted a moment ago. "*Victor* means champion. And that couldn't be further from the truth."

"But you're not Victor."

"That snivelly little bastard? No."

"Can I talk to Victor right now?"

Adrienne could feel his anger before he even stood. She cringed away from him but couldn't get far, lying on the floor with her hands tied. Simon walked over to her, anger suffusing his face. He grabbed her hair and brought his nose inches from hers. Adrienne fought to hold on to consciousness. Having him near was bad enough. Him touching her was unbearable.

"Do you think I'm stupid? That idiot could never do what needs to be done. He never could." Simon jerked her head away from him and released her in disgust.

Adrienne knew she was on dangerous ground. The wrong words said to Simon would send him into a murderous rage.

"Victor couldn't do things right like protect you from *her?*"

Adrienne could feel hesitation in Simon, along with bitterness and fear. He turned from Adrienne and walked back to his perch on the box.

"Auntie always ignored us, and when she wasn't ignoring us, she hurt us," Simon whispered. "We were never good enough for her. She had to be punished."

"But you know those women aren't her, right?"

"But they sound like her and act like her. They hurt and ignore people, like Auntie. They needed to be punished."

"Did the women hurt you?"

"No, but they ignored me when I tried to talk to them, just like Auntie. They mocked me and hated me, just like Auntie."

Adrienne wanted to keep Simon talking as long as possible. "The women made fun of you?"

"Not out loud. But I could tell they were laughing at me inside their heads!"

Adrienne could feel the rage emanating from Simon at the thought of these women mocking and laughing at him.

"But how could you tell, Simon? Did they say mean things to you?"

"No," he scoffed. "They didn't have to. I would try to talk to them and they would just ignore me. But I could see in their eyes that they were laughing at me. All of them."

Adrienne knew trying to further convince Simon of the women's innocence would be futile at best, and possibly deadly for her. She sat silently. You couldn't reason with madness.

"I had to punish them!" Simon continued. "So they

wouldn't hurt other people—just like Auntie. I had to stop them. It was good for me to stop them."

Simon paced back and forth, muttering under his breath. His mind began to calm; evidently he found peace in thinking he was ridding the world of these women.

Adrienne took advantage of the lack of pain and attention from Simon to test the tightness of the rope that tied her hands. Not as tight as she had feared—perhaps she would be able to get them off if she worked at them. But she'd never be able to walk away with the agony of Simon's thoughts filling her head. It was all she could do to stay conscious right now.

But Adrienne still kept working at the bonds—even if she had to crawl away, she could do that.

"Mostly, you're not like them, though. Although you are a little bit because you couldn't even remember Victor's name."

Adrienne could feel Simon's thoughts grow darker.

"I know you're not really like them, but you have to be punished, too, because you're a cheater."

"Didn't you punish me enough when you burnt down my barn?"

The maniacal giggling came again. "That was so much fun! You all looked so inane running around trying to save the silly horses. It was the best entertainment I'd had in a week!"

"I saw you on the porch in the rocking chair," Adrienne muttered through gritted teeth.

"I thought you might have! I'm so glad. You should've come over. We could've chatted."

But Adrienne could see what he would've done to her if she had tried to confront him that night. She definitely would not be alive now. Adrienne shuddered, bile growing in her throat.

"I did mean to kill Agent Harrington," Simon continued. "I must admit I was quite upset he made it out of the barn alive. That was *your* fault."

His rage was back and targeted at her. Adrienne knew she had to do something— right now—but thinking was so hard she couldn't figure out what.

Simon paced back and forth, rubbing his hands together as if he was in deep thought. "Just wanted your opinion on something. I was thinking I would kill you and leave you at the hotel where you first stayed here in San Francisco. Kind of a full circle, don't you agree?" That hideous giggle erupted once more.

Adrienne knew time was running out.

"I think it would be poetic justice for Agent Perigo to find you there, don't you agree?"

"They know who you are now, Simon," Adrienne managed to get out around the pain. "They know what Victor looks like. The FBI has files on him."

Simon stomped his foot like a petulant toddler. "I know! That's so unfair! Now I won't be able to watch as they find you!"

Simon walked toward her and, crouching down, whispered conspiratorially, "That was my favorite part, you know. Watching the FBI process the scenes. Watching them appreciate my handiwork. Knowing they were too stupid to figure out it was me."

Adrienne eased farther away from him. "But they know what you look like. You're going to have to stop. Maybe if you turned yourself in now, they could help you. Maybe you wouldn't even have to go to jail."

Adrienne didn't care what lies she told if it bought

her more time. She knew that was what Conner would want her to do.

Simon wasn't buying it. "No, they don't want to help me. They just want me to stop."

Simon stood and walked across the room to another table. Adrienne watched in terror as he picked up one of the knives on it. He had made his decision; he was going to kill her now. Adrienne knew her time had run out.

She had made some progress getting her wrists loosened, but it didn't matter—the first time he touched her, she would be totally helpless. Her thought process was difficult enough now, and he was across the room.

Whimpering, Adrienne began dragging herself across the floor away from Simon. She heard him laugh and knew he would soon be coming after her. Adrienne tried to stand but collapsed on the floor without even making it to her knees. She began to scoot slowly across the floor again; her limbs were too heavy to move any quicker.

She turned and saw Simon watching her from the table, a knife shining in his hand, smiling with evil glee. "Cheaters never win," he said in his singsongy voice.

It happened so gradually, Adrienne didn't really feel it at first. But instead of being overwhelmed by Simon's thoughts, Adrienne found she could think a little clearer. Looking around her, she saw the door for the first time. She knew that was where she had to get to. She started dragging her body in that direction.

This time when she tried to crawl, her body obeyed. Soon she was able to stumble up onto her feet. She looked over at Simon and could see his surprise that she was able to stand. He was expecting her to fall again.

But Adrienne was able to balance and stay on her feet as she made her way toward the door. She could see the door and Simon clearly. The noise and the pain were leaving.

It came to her then. *Conner.* It had to be Conner. He must be somewhere nearby, blocking her abilities and therefore getting Simon out of her head. She just needed to stay alive for a few more minutes, and Conner would find her.

But Simon didn't look like he was willing to give her a few more minutes. He ran at Adrienne, knife raised in his hand. Adrienne forced herself to stay calm and stepped out of the way as Simon brought the knife down right where she had been standing. She kept her back to the wall and scooted away quickly as Simon advanced on her again.

She could hear a pounding on the door and knew it had to be Conner and Seth.

"Conner!" Adrienne yelled as loudly as she could.

"Adrienne?" she could hear Conner's muffled response before the pounding on the door became more intense. They were trying to break it down.

Adrienne could see the murder in Simon's eyes. Conner and Seth would be too late to help her. She would have to save herself.

Adrienne saw the piece of wood lying on the ground just as Simon rushed her again. When he swung the knife toward her head, she ducked and grabbed the board. As she rose, she swung with all her might, cracking him in the jaw. Simon crumbled at her feet.

A few seconds later the door gave in and Conner and Seth stormed into the building with their weapons raised, obviously ready to take down Simon.

Adrienne could only see Conner. Using the last of her reserves, she stumbled over to him.

"What took you guys so long?" she managed to say as, for the third time in a few days, Adrienne collapsed in Conner's arms.

Chapter Sixteen

"Multiple personality disorder. Unbelievable," Conner muttered. He and Adrienne were back at Conner's town house much later that night. Simon/Victor had been treated for a concussion and broken jaw—thanks to Adrienne—and arrested. Conner and Adrienne had provided statements and had been debriefed, with the promise to be back at the ViCAP offices first thing tomorrow morning.

But multiple personality disorder? Seriously? Well, it certainly explained why Simon/Victor had been able to slip past Adrienne's abilities unnoticed. Evidently Victor had no ill intent toward the women Simon had killed. And the personalities were so separate that Victor had no real knowledge of what Simon was doing.

So he had been around Adrienne all the time but had never given off any ill thoughts to attract Adrienne's abilities. Every once in a while Simon had made his presence known, and those were the times that had hit her the worst and really scared them all.

Conner wasn't certain he believed any of the MPD stuff. He just hoped it didn't end up being the basis for an insanity plea that got Simon off the hook. Too many women had died at the hands of Simon or Victor or whoever you wanted to call him.

And Adrienne had almost been another of his victims.

Conner would never forget those hours of absolute panic when he'd known Simon had Adrienne in his clutches. And those final minutes, trying to get into the building, when he was afraid they weren't going to make it in time. When they got the door open just to see Adrienne crumple to the ground right in front of him, Conner had watched his own world lying broken at his feet.

In that moment it had been crystal clear to him: nothing in his life had any purpose without Adrienne in it.

She sat across from him now, eating a burger they had picked up from a local fast-food place. She looked exhausted—still had dirt on her cheek and some sort of plaster or something in her hair and every bit of makeup had long since worn off.

She was the most beautiful thing he had ever seen.

"I love you." The words were out of his mouth before he had even finished the thought.

Her eyes rounded, and her throat began working up and down. He thought for a second she might be choking and stood up in case she needed help.

"Are you okay?"

Adrienne nodded and finally managed to swallow her food. Conner sat down again. He wasn't expecting the little fist that darted out and punched him in the shoulder. Hard.

"Hey! What was that all about?" Conner complained.

"You're going to make me remember this terrible cheeseburger forever! You're not supposed to say something like that when a girl has a mouthful of greasy food!"

Conner smiled. "Sorry."

"You should be sorry. And I love you, too, Agent Jackass."

"And I want you to marry me."

Adrienne's eyes were wide open again, but this time she didn't have any food in her mouth. Conner knew that less than two weeks wasn't long to know someone. But he had felt more for Adrienne, felt deeper for Adrienne, than he had for anyone in his whole life. He wanted to be with her, to laugh with her, to protect her, to give her the silence she needed whenever she required it.

"Our lives are different," Adrienne finally managed to say.

"But not unblendable. We'll just have to figure out the right balance as we go along. But I want you to know that I don't expect you to come back and work for the Bureau."

Adrienne reached out and stroked his cheek. "I want to help. With you around, I finally think I can." She sighed and pulled away. "But I feel like you give me more than I give you. That it's unequal."

Conner leaned forward and gazed at her intently. "Well, I feel like you give me everything that's important in my life, and I can't live without you. So I'm not sure how we can be unequal."

Adrienne smiled and walked over to his chair. She pushed her finger against his chest until he leaned back, then hiked her legs over his hips so she was sitting astride him. She wrapped her arms around his neck.

"Everything that's important, huh?" she asked. He settled his arms around her hips.

"Every. Single. Thing." Between the words he kissed her, each successive touch of his lips becoming a little deeper, lingering a little longer.

"Well, then, I guess we better get married."

Conner stood up with Adrienne in his arms. "I thought you'd never ask."

* * * * *

COMING NEXT MONTH FROM

H HARLEQUIN®

I N T R I G U E

Available April 15, 2014

#1491 SAWYER
The Lawmen of Silver Creek Ranch • by Delores Fossen

When FBI agent Sawyer Ryland's ex-lover, Cassidy O'Neal, shows up at his family's ranch with a newborn and a crazy story about kidnappers, Sawyer isn't sure what to believe. But he and Cassidy must untangle the secrets and lies and find their future.

#1492 THE DISTRICT
Brody Law • by Carol Ericson

When former lovers Eric Brody and Christina Sandoval follow a serial killer into the occult, their love may be the only weapon to stop the killer.

#1493 LAWLESS
Corcoran Team • by HelenKay Dimon

Hope Algier is unprepared to see her ex, undercover agent Joel Kidd. But when people around her start dying, she's smart enought to lean on the one man she knows can protect them all—Joel.

#1494 SCENE OF THE CRIME: RETURN TO MYSTIC LAKE
by Carla Cassidy

When FBI Agents Jackson Revannaugh and Marjorie Clinton join forces to solve a kidnapping, sparks fly and danger grows near, threatening not only their relationship but also their lives.

#1495 NAVY SEAL SURRENDER
Texas Family Reckoning • by Angi Morgan

Navy SEAL John Sloan must find high school sweetheart Alicia Adams's daughter to clear his estranged twin's name. Can he find the girl without losing his heart?

#1496 THE BODYGUARD
by Lena Diaz

Caroline Ashton has escaped her abusive society husband and hired bodyguard Luke Dawson to protect her from him. But when her husband is murdered, Luke must protect her from the police and a killer on the loose.

YOU CAN FIND MORE INFORMATION ON UPCOMING HARLEQUIN® TITLES, FREE EXCERPTS AND MORE AT WWW.HARLEQUIN.COM.

HICNM0414

REQUEST YOUR FREE BOOKS!
2 FREE NOVELS PLUS 2 FREE GIFTS!

♦HARLEQUIN®
INTRIGUE®

BREATHTAKING ROMANTIC SUSPENSE

YES! Please send me 2 FREE Harlequin Intrigue® novels and my 2 FREE gifts (gifts are worth about $10). After receiving them, if I don't wish to receive any more books, I can return the shipping statement marked "cancel." If I don't cancel, I will receive 6 brand-new novels every month and be billed just $4.74 per book in the U.S. or $5.24 per book in Canada. That's a savings of at least 14% off the cover price! It's quite a bargain! Shipping and handling is just 50¢ per book in the U.S. and 75¢ per book in Canada.* I understand that accepting the 2 free books and gifts places me under no obligation to buy anything. I can always return a shipment and cancel at any time. Even if I never buy another book, the two free books and gifts are mine to keep forever.

182/382 HDN F42N

Name _____ (PLEASE PRINT) _____

Address _____ Apt. # _____

City _____ State/Prov. _____ Zip/Postal Code _____

Signature (if under 18, a parent or guardian must sign)

Mail to the **Harlequin® Reader Service:**
IN U.S.A.: P.O. Box 1867, Buffalo, NY 14240-1867
IN CANADA: P.O. Box 609, Fort Erie, Ontario L2A 5X3
**Are you a subscriber to Harlequin Intrigue books
and want to receive the larger-print edition?
Call 1-800-873-8635 or visit www.ReaderService.com.**

* Terms and prices subject to change without notice. Prices do not include applicable taxes. Sales tax applicable in N.Y. Canadian residents will be charged applicable taxes. Offer not valid in Quebec. This offer is limited to one order per household. Not valid for current subscribers to Harlequin Intrigue books. All orders subject to credit approval. Credit or debit balances in a customer's account(s) may be offset by any other outstanding balance owed by or to the customer. Please allow 4 to 6 weeks for delivery. Offer available while quantities last.

Your Privacy—The Harlequin® Reader Service is committed to protecting your privacy. Our Privacy Policy is available online at www.ReaderService.com or upon request from the Harlequin Reader Service.

We make a portion of our mailing list available to reputable third parties that offer products we believe may interest you. If you prefer that we not exchange your name with third parties, or if you wish to clarify or modify your communication preferences, please visit us at www.ReaderService.com/consumerschoice or write to us at Harlequin Reader Service Preference Service, P.O. Box 9062, Buffalo, NY 14269. Include your complete name and address.

HI13R

SPECIAL EXCERPT FROM

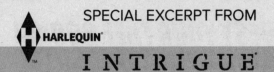

HARLEQUIN®

INTRIGUE

SAWYER
by USA TODAY *bestselling author*
Delores Fossen

A woman he'd spent one incredible night with and the baby who could be his will have Agent Sawyer Ryland fighting for a future he never imagined…

Agent Sawyer Ryland caught the movement from the corner of his eye, turned and saw the blonde pushing her way through the other guests who'd gathered for the wedding reception.

She wasn't hard to spot.

She was practically running, and she had a bundle of something gripped in front of her like a shield.

Sawyer's pulse kicked up a notch, and he automatically slid his hand inside his jacket and over his Glock. It was sad that his first response was to pull his firearm even at his own brother's wedding reception. Still, he'd been an FBI agent long enough—and had been shot too many times—that he lived by the code of better safe than sorry.

Or better safe than dead.

She stopped in the center of the barn that'd been decorated with hundreds of clear twinkling lights and flowers, and even though she was wearing dark sunglasses, Sawyer was pretty sure that her gaze rifled around. Obviously looking for someone. However, the looking around skidded to a halt when her attention landed on him.

"Sawyer," she said.

HIEXP69758

Because of the chattering guests and the fiddler sawing out some bluegrass, Sawyer didn't actually hear her speak his name. Instead, he saw it shape her trembling mouth. She yanked off the sunglasses, her gaze colliding with his.

"Cassidy O'Neal," he mumbled.

Yeah, it was her all right. Except she didn't much look like a pampered princess doll today in her jeans and body-swallowing gray T-shirt.

Despite the fact that he wasn't giving off any welcoming vibes whatsoever, Cassidy hurried to him. Her mouth was still trembling. Her dark green eyes rapidly blinking. There were beads of sweat on her forehead and upper lip despite the half dozen or so massive fans circulating air into the barn.

"I'm sorry," she said, and she thrust whatever she was carrying at him.

Sawyer didn't take it and backed up, but not before he caught a glimpse of the tiny hand gripping the white blanket.

A baby.

That put his heart right in his suddenly dry throat.

*To find out what happens,
don't miss* USA TODAY *bestselling author
Delores Fossen's SAWYER, on sale in May 2014,
wherever Harlequin® Intrigue® books are sold!*

INTRIGUE

TWO FBI AGENTS PUTTING THEIR HEARTS—AND LIVES—ON THE LINE

Only a life-and-death mission could make FBI special agent Jackson Revannaugh leave Louisiana for sultry Kansas. But a husband and wife have gone missing in a case with disturbing similarities to an unsolved one, and Jackson's desperate for answers. If he can keep his taboo desire for his gorgeous new partner from compromising the operation….

Marjorie Clinton knows Jackson's type only too well. But with passion—and the case—heating up, she soon has to trust the Baton Rouge charmer with her life. Because someone in this friendly lakeside town is a killer. Someone who could expose the secret Jackson hoped he'd buried forever.

SCENE OF THE CRIME: RETURN TO MYSTIC LAKE

BY CARLA CASSIDY

Only from Harlequin® Intrigue®.
Available May 2014 wherever books are sold.